DESTRUCTION
OF THE
OVERWORLD

Books by Mark Cheverton

The Gameknight999 Series
Invasion of the Overworld
Battle for the Nether
Confronting the Dragon

The Mystery of Herobrine Series: A Gameknight999
Adventure
Trouble in Zombie-town
The Jungle Temple Oracle
Last Stand on the Ocean Shore

Herobrine Reborn Series: A Gameknight999
Adventure
Saving Crafter
Destruction of the Overworld
Gameknight999 vs. Herobrine (Coming soon!)

The Algae Voices of Azule Series
Algae Voices of Azule
Finding Home
Finding the Lost

AN UNOFFICIAL NOVEL

DESTRUCTION OF THE OVERWORLD

HEROBRINE REBORN
BOOK TWO
<<< A GAMEKNIGHT999 ADVENTURE >>>

AN UNOFFICIAL MINECRAFTER'S ADVENTURE

MARK CHEVERTON

SKY PONY PRESS
NEW YORK

Copyright © 2015 by Mark Cheverton

Minecraft® is a registered trademark of Notch Development AB

The Minecraft game is copyright © Mojang AB

Sky Pony Press books may be purchased in bulk at special discounts
for sales promotion, corporate gifts, fund-raising, or educational
purposes. Special editions can also be created to specifications.
For details, contact the Special Sales Department, Sky Pony Press,
307 West 36th Street, 11th Floor, New York, NY 10018 or info@
skyhorsepublishing.com.

Sky Pony® is a registered trademark of Skyhorse Publishing, Inc.®,
a Delaware corporation.

Visit our website at www.skyponypress.com.

10 9 8 7 6 5 4 3 2 1

Library of Congress Cataloging-in-Publication Data is available on file.

Cover design by Owen Corrigan
Cover artwork by Natalie Cilia
Technical consultant: *Gameknight999*

Print ISBN: 978-1-51070-015-4
Ebook ISBN: 978-1-51070-017-8

Printed in Canada

ACKNOWLEDGMENTS

I'd like to thank my family for their constant support on this literary adventure. Without their help, these books would not have been possible. I'd also like to thank the selfless heroes in my family's life who give to others and expect nothing in return, who have continually supported my writing: Tom and Donna Funiciello, Meg Paolini, Alison and Brandon Seitz, Sharon Crandall, Chad and Lisa Currin, and Kathy Renaud. Also, a big thank-you goes to my editor, Cory Allyn, and the great people at Skyhorse Publishing. Without their hard work, these books would have never made it to the shelves. I'm also grateful to my agent, Holly Root, whose support and advice and friendship has always been deeply valued and appreciated.

Lastly, I'd also like to thank all the kind readers who have been sending me such nice emails through my website, www.markcheverton.com. I love hearing how much you're enjoying reading my books and the impact they are having on your lives. These messages are inspirational, so please keep them coming. I try to answer every one, but I'm sorry if I didn't reply to some because of email errors. Be sure to type your email addresses correctly so I can send back messages. Keep the messages coming!

Don't let fear cloud the vision of who you really are. Fear is important when a tiger or lion or bear (oh my!) is chasing you, but it can keep you from realizing your true self. Just be YOU!

CHAPTER 1
HEROBRINE

The Ender Dragon, infected with Herobrine's virus, flew through The End, his eyes blazing bright white with hatred.

"I will take my revenge on you, Gameknight999," the dragon grumbled to himself as he banked in a huge arc.

Flapping his mighty wings, Herobrine flew toward a tall obsidian tower. A shining ender crystal bobbed about atop the dark purple pillar, a wreath of flames surrounding the intricately carved purple cube. As he neared, a shaft of light lanced out from the crystal and hit the dragon, replenishing his health points (HP) and filling him with energy. Herobrine revealed a vile, toothy grin as he felt himself grow stronger.

Turning, he flew over the End Stone that floated below him, the island of pale yellow blocks completely surrounded by the endless darkness of the void. This was his domain now, and he should have been thrilled to be free of the pig body he'd been trapped in. But instead, being restricted to The End made him feel trapped . . . and furious.

"I hate being here in The End!" Herobrine shouted at the darkness. "I have to escape and make my enemies pay for this."

Looking down, he could see a large collection of endermen clustered together, their black bodies standing out against the insipid yellow End Stone. Suddenly, a new enderman appeared, materializing in a cloud of purple teleportation particles. As the lavender mist cleared, Herobrine recognized the new enderman as different from the rest—colored a dark, dark red, like the color of dried blood. It was his general, Feyd, the king of the endermen.

Swooping down, Herobrine approached the group. Extending his massive wings to slow his descent, the enormous dragon settled gracefully to the ground right in front of the collection of creatures. The endermen all bowed their heads to him immediately, each of them demonstrating the proper respect for the Maker. They all knew that those who had failed to revere him in the past didn't live to make the same mistake twice.

"Maker, what are your commands?" Feyd asked as he stepped forward.

"What did you learn about my enemy, Gameknight999?" Herobrine demanded, his eyes glowing bright white.

"My endermen could not find him, but we are still looking," Feyd replied nervously, afraid to have only bad news for his master.

"I must have him!" Herobrine shouted, his massive teeth mashing together like a mighty vise as he snapped his lethal mouth shut. "He must be found and punished for trapping me in this wasteland. There is nothing to destroy here and it is driving me crazy!"

"I understand," Feyd said carefully, taking a step back.

"The End is like a prison to me," the dragon explained. "I can feel the walls of the void pressing in on me. I cannot stand another minute in this place. I must be free."

Herobrine's eyes blazed even brighter as his rage intensified to dangerous levels.

The endermen around him stepped back even farther, all well aware that it was unsafe to be so close when their maker's eyes grew this intense.

Closing his eyes, Herobrine boiled with anger and hatred.

I have to get out of here somehow. NOW! he thought.

When he was in a normal body, the evil shadow-crafter could teleport anywhere his mind could conceive, and he would have been easily able to leave The End. But in this dragon body, many of his crafting abilities seemed absent . . . or maybe they were just placed somewhere else in his mind.

Concentrating with all his might, Herobrine imagined his body surrounded by purple teleportation particles. With the very fabric of his soul, he willed this to be, searching the crevasses of his mind for the powers he needed.

A tingling spread across his body as though a million tiny little bugs were crawling over his skin.

He ignored the sensation.

Diving even deeper into his mind, Herobrine probed for those lost skills, all the while imagining the field of teleportation particles getting larger and larger. He could sense familiar powers in his mind: the power to change lines of code in other creatures; the ability to hear the music of Minecraft created by that old hag, the Oracle; the ability to change his form when he absorbed another's XP after he'd destroyed them . . .

The tingling grew stronger, now changing from tiny little insects to a million pointed needles, all of them poking into every inch of his skin.

Yes, he could feel many powers, but the one he sought still lay hidden, lost in the recesses of his evil mind. He had to find it! Diving even deeper into his psyche, he probed the darkness of his soul, looking for what he desperately needed: a way out of The End.

The piercing needles turned from an annoyance to genuine pain, and his body felt like it was wrapped in flames. At the same time, Herobrine became dizzy, his mind reeling as though he were wavering back and forth in all directions at once. Most creatures would have felt some kind of fear at this, but Herobrine did not understand what fear was. All he knew was anger and determination.

Suddenly, the dragon had the sensation of being in two places at the same time. It felt like his mind had been severed in half, one part remaining in The End and the other suddenly somewhere else. Herobrine could hear Feyd screeching something, but he did not pay attention to his general; he did not want to be distracted.

Focusing his attention on his inner mind, he suddenly came across something familiar, a power that felt immediately comforting, like an old friend—he'd found it! But just before he could use this power, he was startled by the sound of a cow mooing directly in his face. Opening his eyes, Herobrine found the blocky bovine staring at him only a few blocks away. The dragon lifted his dark head quickly and glanced around at his surroundings, his motion scaring away the cow.

Gasping in shock, Herobrine found himself on a grassy, flower-covered plain. Bright yellow sunflowers surrounded the dragon, their brilliant faces standing out in stark contrast to the lush grass that stretched out into the distance. All around him were tiny, sparkling purple and yellow dots, dancing like an enchanted mist. He immediately recognized them as his teleportation particles and shadow-crafting powers.

A rich birch forest biome butted up against the landscape of sunflowers. The woodland extended out, looking like a gigantic ocean of white-barked trees. Beyond the forest, he could make out some kind of rocky mountain, the tall peaks barely showing through the haze of Minecraft.

Suddenly, a presence appeared before him: Feyd, an eerie smile on the dark face.

"The Maker did it!" the enderman screeched. "You have again done what was thought to be impossible. You teleported out of The End."

Herobrine looked at the enderman, then smiled, realizing what Feyd had said was true. Flapping his mighty wings, the dragon lifted into the air and soared high into the deep blue sky. Laughing with pure joy at being out of his dark prison, Herobrine glided across the landscape, looking for something to destroy. Streaking down to the ground, he found the cow that had mooed at him when he'd first materialized. With his razor-sharp claws extended, Herobrine attacked the cow, his talons rending the HP from the beast. The animal flashed red then disappeared, gone.

Herobrine laughed and flew back toward his general. Now there were more endermen gathering on the grassy plain, their dark bodies like shadowy silhouettes. Settling to the ground before his followers, Herobrine looked at Feyd and smiled maliciously, his white teeth shining bright in the sunlight.

"Friends, it is time to take our revenge on the NPCs of the Overworld," Herobrine snarled, his tail whipping about excitedly, tearing up sunflowers with every twitch. "We will eradicate their infestation and destroy every last one of them!"

The endermen screeched with excitement.

"But Maker," Feyd said, cautiously stepping out of reach. "What of the User-that-is-not-a-user?"

Herobrine growled at the sound of his enemy's name. He stared at Feyd, his eyes glowing bright. "I will have a little surprise for the User-that-is-not-a-user. He will not escape me again." He then looked straight up at the golden square of the overhead sun and shouted into the very fabric of Minecraft: "I'M COMING FOR YOU GAMEKNIGHT999, AND I BRING WITH ME YOUR DOOM!"

CHAPTER 2

GAMEKNIGHT999

Gameknight999 drew back an arrow and aimed at his target. His breathing was slow, his mind calm. He had to focus everything on this shot; he made ever-so-small adjustments to his aim and ignored everything around him. He had to make this shot—everything depended on it.

Stitcher had hit her target with each of her last three arrows. He had to match that. They'd been competing with each other and testing their archery skills, and it had finally come down to these last three arrows.

Once he had quieted his breathing a bit more, he could feel that he had the aim just right. He was about to release his arrow when he saw movement in the forest: something green and splattered with black spots was approaching Stitcher. The young NPC had her back to the forest as she watched Gameknight's target, a pumpkin. It was probably nothing, he thought, and tried to focus once again on the orange striped fruit. But then the mottled intruder moved again through the forest and

Gameknight could see that it was a creeper, and it was getting closer to Stitcher!

Adjusting his aim, he fired, then drew another arrow and fired again and again. His three missiles streaked silently through the air, brushing past square tree trunks and clusters of leaves until they reached their target. The first arrow made the creeper ignite, but the next two quickly disrupted the process and took the creature's remaining HP. It disappeared with a faint *pop*!

He sighed with relief. Stitcher was safe, and she hadn't even noticed the danger lurking behind her.

Moving to the pumpkin, Stitcher laughed aloud. She leaned down, pulled her three arrows out of her pumpkin, and then rubbed the smooth surface of Gameknight's target.

"Looks like you missed all three—I win!" she squealed, jumping up and down, her flowing red curls bouncing like crimson springs.

"That's not fair," Gameknight complained. "There was a—"

"Blah . . . blah . . . blah," mocked Stitcher. "You missed and I didn't. Excuses won't make the arrows hit the target. Admit it: I won and you lost."

Since Stitcher was so happy, Gameknight decided not to spoil the mood and didn't tell her about the creeper. Instead, he moved off into the woods, pretending to sulk. Once he'd located the place where the creeper had disappeared, he collected the glowing balls of XP and gunpowder.

"GAMEKNIGHT . . . WHERE ARE YOU?" a voice shouted through the trees.

Gameknight turned. His father, Monkeypants271, moved through the oak forest. He boasted a monkey's face with big eyes and a wide nose. Fine brown fur ran across his forehead and cheeks, framing a tan oval encircling the eyes, nose, and mouth. This coloration gave him a simian appearance that seemed to make everyone that met him smile.

Or maybe it was his outfit? Superman . . . really?

For some reason, his father had chosen this skin for his character; a monkey dressed in a Superman outfit. A large "S" within a red triangle adorned his chest, a long red cape hung down his back. Blue tights and red boots completed the ensemble. Gameknight shook his head and wondered what his father was thinking when he chose that skin.

"We're over here!" Gameknight shouted, waving his bow high over his head.

As his father approached, Gameknight could tell that he was in trouble by the angry look on the monkey's face.

"I thought we were going to finish the castle!" Monkeypants complained.

"We are," Gameknight replied a little sheepishly, "I just wanted to take a break and go out shooting with Stitcher. I was gonna come back soon."

"That's fine, but you left me with the unpleasant job of building the wall," Monkeypants said. "We collected all that obsidian and now we need to finish the wall of your castle. You know how tedious that can be."

"You could have gotten some of the villagers to help."

"That's not the point," Monkeypants replied. "This was supposed to be something that we were doing together . . . and when the boring parts come, it seems that I'm the only one doing the building."

"I'm sorry. I just wanted to take a little break," Gameknight said, casting his gaze to the ground.

"Remember, we agreed to finish the wall, *then* take a break," Monkeypants reminded his son. "We set a goal and said that we would achieve it before getting distracted by anything else."

"I know . . . but I was getting bored with just placing obsidian blocks," Gameknight whined, "and I wanted to do something else for a while."

"Son, you said that you wanted to be treated like a big kid, like an adult. Part of being an adult is meeting your responsibilities and following through on your commitments. People will trust and respect you, but only if you do what you say and are reliable. So let me ask you: are you a man of your word? When Gameknight999 says he will do something, can others expect that he will follow through, or will they worry that he'll decide to skip it because it isn't fun?"

"Well . . . I . . . um . . ."

"As I've told you before, responsibility is a heavy cloak and requires broad shoulders to support its weight," Monkeypants said. "Are your shoulders strong enough to bear this weight?"

Gameknight scowled as he looked to the ground.

What's the big deal? Gameknight thought. *I just took a little break. Why does he have to make it into a capital offense?*

But he knew that he was wrong and kept his thoughts to himself.

His father had agreed to stay in Minecraft for just a little while longer. He had planned on leaving when they completed Gameknight's castle. At first, Gameknight had been thrilled, but as with all building projects, he quickly became bored with the tedium of getting every detail correct. If they had been regular users simply playing the game, then he could have used hacks and cheats to build his castle faster, but they were not just playing the game—they were *in* the game, for real.

Having learned that Crafter, his best friend in Minecraft, was dying, Gameknight had used his father's invention, the digitizer, to go *into* the game and play it so he could help his friend. He'd done this before, but this time was different. This time, his father had insisted on accompanying him.

Looking at his father now, Gameknight saw the bright letters floating like holograms over his monkey head, displaying his dad's Minecraft name for all users and NPCs to see. It didn't matter from which direction they were viewed, the letters always read, from left to right, *MONKEYPANTS271.* If he had been a regular user, then there would have been a narrow beam of light shining up from the player's head, the server thread. The glowing white filaments connected the users to the server. But because Gameknight999 and Monkeypants271 had used his father's digitizer, or Gateway of Light as the NPCs liked to call it, to enter the game, they had no server threads. They were users without the server thread that all other users had; they were both a User-that-is-not-a-user.

Just then, the music of Minecraft swelled and filled the air. But it wasn't its usual harmonious tones, which normally gave Gameknight999 a sense of serenity and peace. No, there was a dissonant and strained sound to the lyrical notes, as though someone or something were in pain.

"Something's happening!" Gameknight snapped as he notched another arrow to his bow.

Turning away from his father, the User-that-is-not-a-user scanned the forest, looking for any monsters. As far as he could tell, they were still alone.

"Gameknight, don't turn away from me; we were talking," his father complained.

Gameknight ignored Monkeypants and continued to scan their surroundings.

"Don't you hear it?" Gameknight asked.

"Hear what?" his father replied.

"The music of Minecraft," Gameknight answered. "There's something wrong, and the Oracle is giving us a warning through the music."

"Well, I don't hear anything," Monkeypants said.

"I don't hear anything either," Stitcher said, but she too had pulled out her bow again, an arrow notched to the string and drawn back, ready.

"We have to get back to the village," Gameknight said.

"That's what I was saying," Monkeypants said. "We need to finish that wall and then—"

"I think we definitely need to finish that wall," Gameknight said as he continued to peer into the forest. "But we might need the defenses of the castle sooner than we expected. Come on, we need to get the NPCs to finish the upgrades to the walls and defenses all across the village. I fear something terrible has happened in Minecraft and I hate not knowing what it is. We need to talk with Crafter as soon as possible."

Gameknight took off running, wending his way through the forest, keeping his enchanted bow at the ready. Behind him, he could hear Monkeypants and Stitcher. One of them was saying something, but he wasn't paying attention. He was listening to the music of Minecraft.

Oracle, what's happening? he thought, hoping she would answer.

"I hear you, Oracle," Gameknight said aloud to no one. "If you could tell me what's wrong, it would help."

Again, only the harsh music filled his ears.

"What's going on?" Gameknight whispered, sprinting for the village that sat over the next rise.

I'm coming! he thought to the Oracle, his legs pumping with all his strength.

As he ran, he put away his bow and instead drew his old friend, his enchanted diamond sword. Gripping the hilt firmly, he worried about what he might find at his destination.

CHAPTER 3

THE FIRST TO FALL

Herobrine flew high up in the air, his gigantic dark wings riding on the soft breeze that always seemed to be flowing from east to west. Banking and curving about, he glided in a lazy circuitous path, his joyous, evil glare surveying the landscape. He was so happy to be out of the cramped confines of The End that he felt like soaring amongst the clouds forever.

But what he had was never enough. Reaching out with his senses, Herobrine tried to feel how far his new domain extended. Sending his awareness out in all directions, he instantly detected the barrier that surrounded the Overworld—the same one that surround The End—the void.

Below the layer of bedrock, which sat at a build height of zero, he felt the menacing darkness waiting to ensnare anyone foolish enough to dig through this impenetrable layer. He knew the void would be there, but he had not expected it to be looming from above, as well.

Sending his crafting powers high up into the air, Herobrine could feel the cold, heartless barrier trapping him.

He was infuriated.

He climbed, flapping his wings with all his might. Picking up speed as he ascended, Herobrine wanted to punch through this invisible shell. He needed to escape from Minecraft as soon as possible, to free himself from this puny cage, and with the power of the dragon body he now inhabited, it might be possible.

He climbed higher and higher, speeding through the clouds that floated about at layer 130. When he looked down, Herobrine could see his endermen standing on a grassy plain, looking back up at him; they were shadowy specs on a green background, growing smaller and smaller as he climbed.

As he neared the build height, 256 blocks high, Herobrine expected to encounter the intractable barrier, but he found nothing. Below him, the landscape was starting to disappear in a haze, features blurring together into a kaleidoscope of colors and shapes. He accelerated. At a height of 270 blocks, the ground had been completely swallowed in the haze and now only clouds were visible.

He could still feel the void above him, laughing at his efforts.

"We'll see who's laughing when I crash through you," the dragon grumbled.

Flapping his wings harder, he climbed even higher. Now even the boxy shapes of the clouds were shrinking as he ascended. The fluffy white rectangles disappeared when he passed 330 blocks high. Now his only companions were the yellow face of the sun and the blue sky. Higher and higher he went, and yet now his surroundings did not change. After a few minutes worth of enormous effort, Herobrine realized that he could no longer tell if he was moving—he was suddenly suspicious that the void would always be out of reach.

Pausing for a moment, the dragon hovered in the air and glared at his featureless surroundings. Around him, the blue sky looked the same in every direction. Now he doubted if there was even a barrier marking the uppermost edge of his prison. Maybe it was just endless empty space. How could he ever break through this prison wall if he could never reach it?

This thought made him even more frustrated and angry.

Herobrine closed his white, glowing eyes and tried to calm himself. As he focused his mind on extinguishing the flames of rage blossoming within, Herobrine detected the faint tinkle of musical notes just at the edge of his hearing. As he strained to listen, the music became louder and louder. It was the music of Minecraft, and it was laughing at him with its gentle tones and harmonious melodies.

This enraged Herobrine, pushing him beyond rational thought.

The Oracle with her hateful music was mocking him, laughing at his attempts to escape. Herobrine was just as confined as he was in The End, he realized. Being stuck in Minecraft would never be adequate. He could feel the freedom of the Internet just on the other side of the void, but now he felt doomed. He would never break through and escape.

He was truly trapped!

"Grrrr!" the dragon growled, then yelled at the fabric of Minecraft. "You want to keep me trapped in this server? Fine! Let me show you the kind of damage I can do!"

Tucking his wing into his side, Herobrine dove straight for the ground. Pulling in his front and back paws, he turned his body into a dark, scaly missile. The wind howled as he plummeted to the earth. Quickly, the clouds became visible again, then the ground emerged from the haze, both growing larger as he fell. When he pierced the fluffy clouds, Herobrine extended his arms and legs, slowing himself just a bit. He then opened his wings slowly, reducing his speed. Banking, he spiraled to the ground, circling in great wide arcs, eyes blazing with fury. He saw tiny dark specs moving about on the terrain, some of them wrapped in a purple haze: his endermen. From this altitude, they were just the smallest of black spots, but he knew they were watching and waiting for him. As he circled, Herobrine thought he saw something in the distance, a shape he recognized. When he curved around, he looked again.

And there it was—the outline of a tall cobblestone tower. It was a village; a delicious, harmless, unprotected village. Perfect!

"Behold my wrath!" the dragon yelled at the still chiming musical notes.

Curving in a great arc, Herobrine approached his host of monsters, silently gliding over the treetops until he was upon them. Flapping his wings once, he hovered in the air for just an instant then settled atop a tall spruce. Herobrine glared down at his dark warriors, his eyes glowing bright with frustration and rage. The Maker could see there were likely fifty of them here in the Overworld, and he knew there were another hundred still in The End. He would call for the others when he needed them, but that would not be today. Fifty was easily enough to erase that village in the distance.

"I have found our first target," bellowed the dragon. "A village lies to the east. It will be the first victim in our campaign of retribution."

The endermen screeched in excitement.

"Feyd, lead your warriors forward," Herobrine said. "We will punish these NPCs for their defiance. You know what to do."

"It will be done," Feyd screeched, then teleported away, the endermen following their general.

Leaping into the air, Herobrine climbed high as he beat his leathery wings. Reaching a height of a dozen blocks in seconds, he curved to the east and flew toward the distant village. His endermen didn't bother to walk the distance. Instead they just disappeared, materializing twenty blocks from where they'd been, again and again, always moving to the east. Herobrine smiled as he watched his shadowy warriors zip across the landscape. From this height, they looked like tiny bolts of black lightning, Feyd like a deadly bolt of dark crimson.

Soon, they passed out of the forest and into a savannah biome. The gray-green grass of the new landscape marked a clear transition from the lush green foliage of the spruce forest. Herobrine smiled at the bent acacia trees. Their gray bark looked sad and almost lifeless compared to the mighty spruces they'd just seen. Like tortured souls, every tree was distorted in a different way, giving the impression that they were writhing in distress.

Herobrine loved this biome.

Brown and white cows walking about munched on the grass covering the ground. The harmless animals wandered across the countryside, ignorant of the approaching tide of destruction. The endermen had to dodge the cows, making sure they didn't materialize inside one of the annoying bovines. Herobrine wanted to fly down and destroy some of the pathetically peaceful animals, but he suppressed the urge; he had more important things to do.

Through the haze, the cobblestone watchtower was starting to show its stony face. As he neared, more of the village became visible. A tall stone wall surrounded the community, protecting the collection of wooden structures and inhabitants. Unfortunately for the NPC builders, they had not planned on the Ender Dragon's visit.

Bellowing a mighty roar, Herobrine accelerated toward the village. He flew around the community, making sure all of the villagers could see him. Panic and terror blossomed within the hearts and minds of the NPCs. He could hear cries of disbelief as they looked up at the Ender Dragon, their shouts of fear making the flying monster smile with joy.

Streaking down to the stone barricade, Herobrine flung his tail into the structure, smashing through a wall and tearing a huge gash into the fortification. His endermen didn't really need the wall removed, for they had already begun teleporting inside the village walls. He simply wished to scare the villagers a little more. He needed them in a panic for his plan to work.

"Teleport into the village, my endermen," roared Herobrine. "Attack the cowards who do not resist!"

Villagers drew their weapons, ready to fight, but all were petrified with fear. Most knew they could not engage the dark endermen, for attacking one would enrage all. Many of the villagers just looked to the ground, shaking with fear. But then Herobrine saw a young boy, his body between that of a child and a man. Feyd, too, saw the youth and teleported to him, a terrifying chuckle coming from the king of the endermen. With a scowl, the young NPC swung his blade at the tall monster. Feyd did not teleport away; he merely shifted to the side so the weapon would score a glancing hit, doing less damage but still causing him to flash red. Like the whistle on a nightmarish freight train, a piercing screech emanated from the endermen king, causing all the NPCs to put boxy hands over their ears. The endermen all across the battlefield shook as their toothy mouths opened, their eyes glowing bright white. Now enraged, all the endermen struck back with lightning speed, hammering the ignorant villagers with fists of fury.

Herobrine smiled as he watched.

Looking across the village, he could see more endermen joining the fray, Feyd's cry of pain enraging the other shadowy monsters. Moving in a black blur, the endermen teleported, attacking NPC after NPC, sparing none. Some villagers bolted for the cobblestone watchtower, likely trying to escape on the minecart network that wove through Minecraft. Others ran out of the gaping hole in the village wall, running for their lives.

"Let a few of them go!" bellowed Herobrine as endermen moved to cut them off. "They will tell the other villages what has happened here. Their panic will grow when they hear of the unstoppable enderman army."

The villagers bolted past the dark creatures and shot into the watchtower, slamming the door behind them. The last living NPCs sprinted away from the village and out into the wilderness. They would likely not survive, but their chances were better than staying and battling endermen and the Ender Dragon. In a minute, the sounds of battle had grown silent, the village now empty of living inhabitants.

Looking about at all the items strewn on the ground, Herobrine laughed.

"A great battle," Feyd said to his master. "Should we now return to The End?"

"Return? Never!" snapped Herobrine.

"But we must—"

"This victory did not satisfy me," the Maker replied. "There are still many more villages out there to destroy. And yet, somehow even the thought of destroying *all* the villages in the Overworld will not be enough."

Before him sat the items from the village crafter: potions, tools, crafting bench, weapons, and armor lay bobbing on the ground, discarded. The crafter had been wielding a diamond sword, which had hurt some of his endermen. The sword reminded Herobrine of something—or someone.

Suddenly, an image of his mortal enemy appeared in his mind. It made him growl with anger. Feyd took a step away from the dragon.

"*That's* what I must destroy," Herobrine said aloud to no one, to everyone.

"What?" Feyd asked. "Maker, what is your plan?"

Herobrine flapped his wings and moved to the roof of the blacksmith's shop, then glared down at his endermen, his eyes like two brilliant suns.

"Friends, today is the start of a great invasion," Herobrine bellowed. "My endermen will cleanse the Overworld and rid Minecraft of the pathetic NPCs.

And after we have emptied the world of these puny beings, we will focus our retribution onto our true enemy, Gameknight999."

The endermen screeched in excitement.

Herobrine leapt into the air and climbed high overhead. He then arced around and flew low over the heads of his endermen. Flapping his leathery wings in a smooth rhythm, he hovered just over their dark heads.

"Come, my friends. We must find the next village, then the next and the next, until all of Minecraft is wiped clean!" the dragon roared.

The monster, infected with the most evil virus to have ever existed, then looked down at his endermen king. "Feyd, we will need more monsters. We cannot rely on the foolish villagers being stupid enough to strike one of your endermen so that they can join the fight. We need more monsters, different monsters. Make it happen!"

"I must find the zombie-town where Xa-Tul, king of the zombies, hides. It may take some time," the king of the endermen said.

"Don't give me excuses!" roared the dragon. "I want results! Just get it done. I'm sure you can wring information out of the idiotic zombies and easily locate their ruler. Do what you must, but we need his zombies!"

Feyd looked up at the Maker and then bowed low. Smiling knowingly, the dark red enderman gathered his teleportation powers and disappeared in a cloud of purple mist.

Herobrine glanced at the rest of his endermen army and growled in approval. He then let his thoughts drift off to his enemy, Gameknight999. The idea of facing the User-that-is-not-a-user in his current dragon form made him almost giddy with evil anticipation.

"I can't wait to meet you again, Gameknight999!" the dragon yelled as he circled higher up into the air so that he could look down upon the world he was about to conquer.

CHAPTER 4
THE VILLAGE

Gameknight worried as he ran through the forest. Ahead, the dense trees were thinning out and a grassy plains biome was just beyond.

Good . . . we're almost home, he thought.

When he reached the edge of the forest, he paused to catch his breath. At his side, he found Stitcher, the young NPC's red curly hair matted with sweat. Two steps behind him was his father, the monkey's superman cape billowing as he ran.

"Were you going to keep running forever?" Stitcher asked between panting breaths.

"There's something going on in Minecraft and I need to get back to Crafter," Gameknight999 explained.

Suddenly the discordant music of Minecraft swelled again. Frowning, the User-that-is-not-a-user looked at Stitcher. She too had a scowl painted across her square brow.

"You hear it too?" Gameknight asked.

Stitcher nodded her head, her deep brown eyes filled with worry.

"What is it?" she asked.

Gameknight shook his head. "I don't know, but we need to find out."

He looked at Monkeypants.

"Do you hear it?" Gameknight asked.

"I can now," his father replied, "and it doesn't sound good. This Oracle of yours must be battling some new threat."

The Oracle was an artificially intelligent antivirus program that had been loaded into Minecraft after the Herobrine-virus had infected the servers. But they had destroyed that terrible monster in The End, and Gameknight couldn't imagine what could be battling with the Oracle, unless . . .

No . . . it's not possible, Gameknight thought. *I saw him fall into the void. Herobrine is dead. It must be something else.*

Across the grassy plain, Crafter's village stood tall and magnificent. A high stone wall ringed the community and a deep watery moat curved farther out. Across the moat, a wooden bridge led to the village gates. Next to the bridge, twin cobblestone towers stood upon which archers waited, ready—always ready.

Off to the right was a new addition: Gameknight999's castle. A half-completed obsidian wall surrounded a large rectangular stone keep that loomed high in the air. Rocky crenellations adorned the top of the stone structure, the alternating blocks giving archers some protection during battle. Jutting out of the sheer walls were numerous torch-lit balconies, each with iron bars encircling the small terraces. Archer towers soared high over the incomplete obsidian walls. The stone structures extended upward and then out over the wall, giving them an unobstructed field of fire out onto the battlefield. Holes were visible on the floor of the cantilevered structures, allowing warriors to shoot straight down at those who might be trying to breach the iron gates.

Around the base of the incomplete obsidian wall, Gameknight could see Grassbrin—one of the light-crafters—placing tall grass, the long leafy plants likely intended to ensnare any monster who moved too close. On the plain in front of the castle, the other light-crafter, Treebrin, was planting tall spruces and oaks, forming a narrow path any approaching enemy would have to take. This would force the attacking foe to cluster together when they approached the castle, limiting the advantage of a larger army and making them easier to hit with arrows. Through the opening of the incomplete wall, Gameknight could also see a string of oak trees planted throughout the courtyard, the trees spanning the distance between the wall and the keep. He knew the light-crafter had placed these trees in a careful arrangement so they could be climbed quickly to gain access to the top of the walls. They would also provide a supply of apples for food.

Gameknight had been thrilled when the light-crafters had offered to help. He had wanted to build this castle with his father and politely refused the help of the other villagers. But the User-that-is-not-a-user had formed a close friendship with the two strange light-crafters, and his father had not minded their inclusion.

Gameknight smiled as he looked down upon his castle. It far exceeded anything he could have built on his own. In the design, they had put to use his father's bizarre knowledge of medieval castles and fortifications, creating arrow slits for more archers, hoarding holes from which water could be poured on any attacking army, and a complex system of tunnels and holes to ensnare the unwary. Monkey-pants had thought of every possible defense for the castle and built it into the structure, not because they were expecting an attack (after all, Herobrine had been defeated), but because it put a smile on his son's face.

Looking at the incomplete obsidian wall, Game-knight now felt guilty. He had ignored his responsi-bility and left his father to do the tedious work and that had been wrong. Just as he had been about to say something to his father, Monkeypants ran off toward the village.

"Come on, son," his father called out. "I don't like the sound of that music. Your Oracle must be in trouble."

"Yeah, let's go, Gameknight," Stitcher added with a smile. "You don't want your dad beating you to the village, do you?"

Flashing her a scowl, the User-that-is-not-a-user sprinted forward, catching up with his father. As they neared the village, Gameknight could see NPCs moving to the defenses: archers crossed the bridges from the fortified wall to occupy the archer towers and warriors moved to stand atop the tall barricade.

Something was happening.

Looking over his shoulder, Gameknight scanned the terrain for the presence of monsters, but he saw none. The User-that-is-not-a-user glanced in Stitcher's direction as he ran and saw a look of concern on her young face; she had the same con-fused thoughts running through her mind.

Suddenly, the iron doors leading into the village burst open. A squad of cavalry burst forth, the horses and riders all wearing iron armor, some of them decorated with bright colors—a remnant of his sister Monet113's artistic touch.

Monet, you see the armor? Gameknight thought, his words flying out to the chat.

I do, it looks cool, she typed back.

His sister Jenny was sitting back in their basement in the physical world. She had not come *into* the game with Gameknight and their father, rather she was watching their progress on the computer, ready to give aid if needed.

It seems like you not only had an effect on the zombies in Zombie-town with your art, but also on some of the NPCs here in the village, he thought.

Gameknight could sense, somehow, that she was smiling.

The horsemen and horsewomen rode across the wooden bridge spanning the moat then split off into smaller groups. Each cluster of warriors went in a different direction to scout the surroundings.

Gameknight ran across the bridge and into the village. He found NPCs hustling in all directions, preparing for battle by putting arrows in chests and food near the defenders in case they were wounded. As he ran through the commotion, no one spoke a word or acknowledged his presence. This village was full of seasoned warriors who had been attacked numerous times by the monsters of Minecraft; all of them knew their jobs and were serious about performing them to the best of their abilities.

Gameknight ran past multiple wooden buildings, following the gravel paths that served as walkways. As he ran past the village's well, he saw NPCs lowering buckets into the stony ring; water had proven to be a powerful defensive tool in the past.

He could smell the furnaces working overtime as he streaked past the blacksmith's shop. Plumes of smoke rose from the dark cubes, the fire within lighting the bottom half with flickering orange flames. As he moved by, Gameknight saw Smithy withdraw stacks of iron ingots and hand them off to one of the crafting chamber workers. The NPC took the load of metal and ran toward the tall cobblestone tower that sat at the center of the village. Gameknight reached the door of the watchtower first and held it open for the worker. The blocky character quickly shot through and stepped to the secret tunnel, which was already open, and disappeared down a long vertical ladder. Gameknight followed close behind him.

In a minute, Gameknight999 had traversed the tunnels and reached the entrance to the crafting chamber. The iron doors stood open. Stopping to take a breath, the User-that-is-not-a-user could hear the banging of hammers, the bending of metal, and the splintering of wood. When Monkeypants271 and Stitcher reached his side, they walked into the chamber together.

Below him, Gameknight could see every person working hard at a crafting bench. Weapons were spilling out onto the floor: swords, armor, bows, arrows . . . all the tools of war slowly formed mounds beside each bench. NPCs ran throughout the chamber, gathering the items and placing them into chests. The entire scene reminded Gameknight of a beehive, with each worker knowing his task and moving without thought or word to complete his job.

And then he spotted Crafter right in the center of everything. The young NPC stood out in his black smock, a wide gray stripe running down the center. He was directing the workers as needed. Gameknight ran down the curving steps and moved to his best friend's side.

"Crafter, something is going on," Gameknight blurted out. "The Oracle, she is—"

"Yes, I heard the music, we all did," Crafter replied.

"I don't like it. Something is going on," Gameknight said.

"Well, until the enemy shows itself, all we can do is prepare," Crafter explained.

"You don't think we should send riders out into the minecart network to warn the other villages?" Gameknight asked, a little surprised that his friend wasn't as troubled by the changing music as he was.

Throughout the crafting chamber ran a series of minecart tracks, the iron rails weaving a complex, winding path, each moving past as many crafting benches as possible and then disappearing into dark tunnels. The tracks moved throughout Minecraft, connecting all the villages and temples together in an intricate spiderweb-like network, keeping everyone connected. The network was invisible to users; it was one of the many great secrets of Minecraft. When sections of the network did become visible, workers would disguise the tracks as old abandoned mines, leaving behind chests filled with supplies and treasure. The network would then be rerouted around the visible section, keeping the connection between villages and temples.

"No, Gameknight, I think it's best we prepare for now," Crafter said. "Once we are ready for battle, we will send out riders. But more importantly, we should—"

Suddenly, commotion sounded at the entrance of the crafting chamber. Glancing up at the iron doors, Gameknight999 could see Hunter bounding down the steps, two-at-a-time, sprinting toward the pair. She was in full iron armor and likely had been one of the cavalry that went out to scout the surroundings.

When she reached their side, she stopped to catch her breath.

"Hunter, is everything alright?" Monkeypants asked.

Holding up a hand, she took a deep breath. She took another as she removed her iron helmet. Scarlet curls burst out, spilling down her shoulders and back. In the torchlight, her hair seemed to almost glow with magical power.

Gameknight smiled.

"Hunter, are you OK?" Stitcher asked, her own hair matching her sister's in luster and beauty.

"Yeah, I'm OK," Hunter finally replied. "I sprinted here from the gates after riding through the forest. I was just a little out of breath."

"You have news?" Crafter asked.

"Yes, we found something. Well, not something but someone," she explained. "You all have to come up and hear what they have to say."

"Is it bad news?" Crafter asked.

Hunter laughed grimly. "When have I ever brought good news?" she asked.

"Not very often," Gameknight said.

"True then," Monkeypants said, a look of pride on his face.

"Daaad," Gameknight whined. "It's not 'true then,' it's 'true dat!' You're embarrassing me."

"True dat!" Hunter echoed with a smile. "Now all of you—come on, you have to hear their story."

Hunter spun and streaked back up the steps, her sister fast on her heels. Crafter bolted after the sisters, leaving Gameknight and his father on the chamber floor. Monkeypants flashed his son a goofy smile, then followed the NPCs, his long red cape flowing behind him, giving the impression that he was flying. Rolling his eyes, Gameknight followed as trepidation filled his mind.

CHAPTER 5

THE LOST

They were met with a confusing scene when they emerged from the cobblestone watch-tower. All the villagers were standing in a large crowd, surrounding a lone NPC. She was eating a slice of melon and was then handed an apple and a loaf of bread. As Gameknight pushed through the crowd, he gained a better view of the villager. By the look of her clothing, he guessed she was a farmer; she wore a light brown smock, a dark brown stripe running down the center. Her hair was the silver gray of a person that had seen many years in Minecraft, her face wrinkled, her hands worn. This was probably the oldest NPC any of them had ever seen.

She was sitting on a block of stone someone had placed on the ground. She was obviously exhausted, likely having been near starvation when she was found. When she saw Hunter approach, she smiled and stood on unsteady legs to gave her a big hug.

"Thank you again," Farmer said, her voice old and scratchy. "If you hadn't found me, I would have died out there."

"You are welcome here, Farmer," Crafter said as he pushed his way through the crowd. "I am this village's crafter, and you are no longer a Lost. This is your new home."

Farmer looked down at the diminutive NPC, a look of confusion on her face. When her eyes drifted to his clothing, she saw the black smock and gray strip of a crafter. Smiling, a look of relief came across her square face, her hazel eyes brightening with hope.

"Thank you so much," she said. With her back bent with age and her old legs wobbling, she reached out and wrapped her tired arms around Crafter. Releasing the hug, Farmer looked down at him. "Only a few of us survived. I ran out into the wilderness knowing that I was Lost, but that was better than staying and being destroyed. I knew someone of my age had little chance of survival, but being Lost was better than the alternative."

"What happened?" Crafter asked.

Farmer sat down and terrible memories returned to her.

"We were attacked . . . my village was destroyed."

"Attacked? By whom?" Gameknight asked.

Farmer stared at the ground for a moment, then slowly raised her gray head and looked at Gameknight999. Mouthing the glowing letters that floated over his head, she realized he was a user, but then her eyes drifted to the air above his head. She instantly recognized who he was when she did not see the server thread—the User-that-is-not-a-user. Farmer's eyes grew wide with surprise.

"Endermen," she said, her voice sounding like sandpaper scratching wood.

A gasp came from the villagers.

"An enderman attacked your village?" Game-knight asked.

"No, not *an* enderman," Farmer replied. "Many endermen!"

"Great, not just one enderman, but lots of them," Hunter said. "This just gets better and better."

"Hunter, be quiet and listen," Stitcher reprimanded. The younger sister rolled her eyes at the older while Stitcher said, "Please, Farmer, ignore my rude sister."

The old farmer sighed and continued.

"They came out of the west. It was a few days ago . . . a normal day like any other, but then suddenly they were there at our walls. Watcher sounded the alarm and we ran to our battle positions but then it slashed through our walls, and the gaping hole let the monsters just walk in."

"How did they destroy your wall?" Crafter asked. "Was it made of dirt or wood?"

"Of course not!" Farmer snapped. "Our crafter would not have been that stupid. We know that endermen can take naturally occurring blocks. We used cobblestone—something that they cannot remove."

"Then what destroyed your village wall?" Game-knight asked.

She sighed again, then stood and looked at all the NPCs around her.

"They destroyed everyone in the village without a single thought of mercy," she said, her voice cracking with emotion. "Men, women, and children were snuffed into nonexistence as if they didn't matter. My family was destroyed—my husband, my daughters . . . my grandsons . . ."

Tiny square tears flowed down her rectangular wrinkled cheeks as the memories of her deceased family overcame her. Reaching a hand high into the air, Farmer spread her fingers wide and then clenched them into a fist; it was the salute to the dead. The villagers around her saw the anguish on her face and did the same, raising their hands out of respect and then clenching their boxy fingers into angry, vengeful fists.

Slowly, Farmer lowered her hand and looked up at Gameknight999, grief filling her eyes. The User-that-is-not-a-user reached out and placed a reassuring hand on her shoulder.

"You are safe now; we won't let anything hurt you here," he said.

She nodded her head.

"You said something destroyed your fortified wall," Crafter asked. "What was it?"

In a low voice, almost a whisper, she said, "The Ender Dragon."

"The Ender—" Hunter started to exclaim, but was silenced by a rueful look from Stitcher.

"How can the Ender Dragon be here in the Overworld?" Monkeypants asked. "I thought we killed that monster. And besides, they are only supposed to be in The End . . . right?"

"That's correct," Crafter said. "But whenever an Ender Dragon dies, an egg is produced to allow a new one to be born, maintaining balance within Minecraft."

"We don't care about balance!" snapped Hunter.

"That may be true, but this is the way Minecraft works," Crafter replied. "Balance keeps all the systems working together."

"Balance should have kept an Ender Dragon out of the Overworld," Hunter growled.

"An Ender Dragon in the Overworld," Gameknight said, grimacing. "This must be why the music sounded as if it were in pain."

"What do we do?" Stitcher asked, looking from Crafter to Gameknight999.

"First we go to Farmer's village and see if anyone needs help," Crafter explained. "And then we find this Ender Dragon and have a little talk with him."

"Just what I want to do—have a chat with a dragon," Hunter said sarcastically. "Sounds like it will be very productive."

"We'll take a small group in case some of the endermen are watching our village," Gameknight said.

"I'm going with you," Farmer said, her scratchy voice filled with determination. "This is my village and I won't abandon anyone who might need help."

Gameknight nodded his head then turned and faced Crafter. "Let's get this done. Everyone get ready. We have a dragon that needs tending!"

The villagers exploded into motion. Groups of NPCs collected horses and supplies while others went into chests to equip Farmer. Gameknight watched with appreciation as the community moved into action like a well-oiled machine. Gameknight examined everyone around him, but looked for one in particular.

"Herder! Where's Herder?" Gameknight shouted.

"Right here," said a voice from directly behind him.

The lanky boy was standing almost on top of him. Gently pushing him back a step, Gameknight smiled. At Herder's side was a wolf, its white fur bright and clean in the sunlight.

"Herder, I want you to bring some wolves with us," Gameknight said. "I'm not sure what we will run into, so I'd rather be prepared."

The skinny boy stood tall with pride.

"I'll bring my best," he said as he spun around and headed for the pack that stood guard around the animal pens.

"Hurry," Gameknight shouted, and the boy ran away, his long black hair bobbing up and down with each step.

The User-that-is-not-a-user moved to the village gates and stepped outside. He found his father standing on the wooden bridge extending over the moat and took a spot by his side. Before them stretched a grassy plain, and a forest lay just beyond.

"Are you up for another adventure?" Gameknight asked. "I think the villagers could use our help."

Monkeypants turned and looked at his son. "I don't know, son. This could be dangerous work."

"But they are my friends, and it's my responsibility to help them," Gameknight replied. "You just told me that I shouldn't ignore my responsibilities just because they're inconvenient. These people rely on the User-that-is-not-a-user not only to help them, but also to give them hope. What kind of signal would it send if I snuck away right when they needed me?"

His father considered his words and smiled.

"You'll have to put up with me some more if you intend to go on this odyssey," Monkeypants said. "Your responsibility may be to protect these villagers, but my responsibility is to make sure you are safe, and it turns out that's a full-time job when you're running around in Minecraft. So if you want to go on this adventure . . . then I'll be right at your side the whole time."

Gameknight smiled and nodded his head.

"Let's go help our friends," the User-that-is-not-a-user said in a strong, confident voice.

"True dat!" replied his father.

CHAPTER 6

THE SCENE OF THE CRIME

They rode out at dawn, not wanting to get caught out in the open after nightfall. The party consisted of Gameknight, his friends, and warriors handpicked by Digger. Farmer led the way, retracing her steps back along her terrified flight from her village. She took the party through the forest that sat before Crafter's village, and then a mega taiga biome on the other side, reaching the savannah that lay beyond.

As they entered the unusual gray-green landscape, Gameknight always marveled at the strange distorted trees. Each one was bent and twisted at a different angle, as if bowing in some kind of invisible howling hurricane.

"I love this biome," Gameknight said to Hunter, who galloped at his side. "All the trees look fantastic."

"I like it too," she replied. "With the trees spread out, I can see an enemy coming from far away." She pointed to the left with her shimmering bow. "Those spiders trying to hide in the treetops? They're easy to see out here."

Gameknight peered into the distance. Two large black shapes sat atop one of the deformed acacia trees, trying to hide in the foliage, but their dark furry bodies stood out against the grayish leaves, making them easy to spot—and avoid.

"It's just over this next hill," Farmer called out over her shoulder.

She was riding at the front of the group next to Crafter. Gameknight kicked his mount to a sprint and moved up next to his friend, the horse's iron armor jangling and clanking. Holding the reins with one hand, he drew his own enchanted bow and readied himself for battle.

"You think the endermen are still there?" Gameknight asked nervously.

"I doubt it," Crafter replied. "What use would they have for a village? They don't need the shelter or the crops, and they certainly don't need the livestock. No, this was not an attack based on any kind of need—it was one of malice and spite."

"You're making us all feel much better," Hunter added sarcastically.

"There it is," Farmer said as they crested the hill.

In the distance, Gameknight could see a village nestled amidst the crooked acacia trees. A tall cobblestone wall surrounded a cluster of wooden buildings and a watchtower loomed high at the center. It all looked normal and as Gameknight would have expected . . . except for the massive gash in the protective barricade. A gigantic section of the wall was completely missing, as though some giant had swiped at the fortification with a steel fist. Hundreds of blocks of cobblestone lay bobbing up and down on the ground, floating just above the pale grass—the remnants of the destruction.

Slowing to a walk, the party approached the silent village cautiously.

Monkeypants rode alongside his son. "What are those things floating on the ground just inside the wall?" Monkeypants asked.

Gameknight looked to where his father was pointing and saw swords, picks, shovels, food, armor, potions . . . items of every type floated on the ground, just like the blocks of cobblestone.

"Those are the belongings of the villagers who once lived here," Gameknight replied.

"What do you mean? They just left them there when they ran away?" Monkeypants271 asked.

"No . . . that's where they dropped them when they died," Farmer replied as she glanced toward the monkey. "Those were my family and friends' belongings. Now they are the only things that prove they ever existed."

Gameknight looked toward the woman and could see burning rage in her old, wrinkled eyes. It was the kind of hatred that had almost consumed Hunter when her family was destroyed by Malacoda and his monsters from the Nether long ago. Now the pattern was repeating.

"Herder, it may be best if you sent in your wolves to investigate for us," Crafter suggested.

The lanky boy nodded his head, then bent down and whispered something to the alpha male. The wolf barked once, then sprinted off with the rest of the wolves following. As the animals moved forward, they reminded Gameknight of the time they had rescued Hunter from Malacoda's clutches. Herder's wolves had saved the day during that battle, as they had many times after.

The wolves ran toward the silent village and shot through the opening in the tall cobblestone wall, quickly disappearing behind what remained of the wall. In less than a minute, the pack leader appeared at the opening and barked once, signaling it was safe.

"Wait here," Digger said to the others.

Kicking his dark horse forward, the big NPC motioned to a couple of the warriors. The small group sprinted forward, moving quickly into the village, swords drawn. As they took up guarding positions around the entrance, they scanned the surroundings, then confirmed the wolf's assertion: it was indeed safe.

The rest of the party galloped into the village. Hunter and Stitcher instantly rode for the watchtower. Gameknight watched as the siblings dismounted and shot up into the cobblestone structure. In seconds, they appeared at the top of the tower and surveyed their surroundings.

"No endermen nearby," shouted Hunter. "It's all clear."

"Search all the houses—quick," Crafter shouted.

The NPCs spread out through the village, peering in every dwelling. Most were empty, but some had items floating on the ground within the wooden structures; the villagers had been destroyed within their own homes.

"Should we collect the items we find?" a warrior named Builder asked.

"Nothing goes to waste in Minecraft," Digger replied. "Collect everything and—"

"No!" snapped the User-that-is-not-a-user. He could see the pain on Farmer's face as she looked at the floating items. "They serve a greater purpose as markers for the terrible thing that happened here. Let all who come to this village witness what occurred and remember those who were lost."

Raising his hand, fingers spread wide, Gameknight looked at the other NPCs, then clenched his hand into a fist. Squeezing it tight, he closed his eyes and imagined the terror the villagers must have experienced. The senseless violence that had crashed down upon these souls filled Gameknight999 with a burning rage.

These people did not deserve this, he thought. *When will the violence end?!*

A growl escaped his mouth, a sound that held all of his anger and frustration at this horror. Another growl sounded next to him, then another and another. Opening his eyes, Gameknight found that the wolves had surrounded him. The creatures were staring at the items on the ground with teeth bared, snarls echoing in their throats, fur bristling with anger.

"They feel your rage," Herder said from behind.

Gameknight turned and slowly lowered his fist. The User-that-is-not-a-user knelt and patted the largest wolf on the back, stroking his white fur, then stood and looked at his friends.

"We will bring those responsible for this to justice," Gameknight whispered to the wolf. "I promise you that."

The wolf looked up at Gameknight999 and understanding seemed to flash through its dangerous red eyes before its bristling fur lay down, relaxed again. Gameknight patted the animal once more, then turned and faced Digger.

"We need to get to the crafting chamber," the User-that-is-not-a-user said. "There may be survivors there. Herder, have the wolves protect the watchtower. Come on everyone."

Turning from the sad items, he sprinted for the watchtower, the other NPCs trailing a few steps behind. As he entered, Gameknight found Hunter already descending down the long ladder, her crimson locks just disappearing into the darkness. He quickly followed, mounting the rungs and sliding down into the underground tunnels, Digger close behind. With his heart pounding, he sprinted through the tunnels and into the large subterranean chamber. Just like the village above, he found the crafting chamber was strewn with items: tools, food, chests . . . the belongings of the dead.

Gameknight felt a tear seep from the corner of his eye. It was not a tear of sadness, though he *was* incredibly sad. No, this was a tear formed from an overwhelming rage that burned within Gameknight999 like an inferno. Wiping the tear away with his sleeve, he took the steps two at a time, running to the chamber floor. Hunter and Stitcher were already there, but the sisters were just standing, looking at the items strewn across the floor. Gameknight guessed they were imagining the horror that had occurred here, the terror the villagers must have felt in their final moments.

Suddenly, a sound came from one of the tunnels. In a fluid motion, both sisters pulled out their bows, notched their arrows, and aimed at the source of the sound; a dark tunnel opening. Digger pulled out his iron pickaxe and approached the tunnel cautiously, two warriors at his side.

Drawing his enchanted diamond sword, Gameknight walked closer. The blue iridescent light from his sword added to that from his enchanted armor, casting a sapphire circle of illumination. As he approached, some of the light spilled into the tunnel, showing the faint outline of a villager. Gameknight took a step closer and saw an NPC, a look of terror painted on his face.

Gameknight put away his sword and held out a hand to the individual to show he meant no harm.

"Come out; we're here to help," Gameknight said.

The villager poked his head out of the shadowy passage and looked at the other NPCs, then cautiously stepped out of the tunnel. By his clothes, Gameknight could see that he was a cobbler; his smock was a rich sky-blue with a gray stripe running from neck to hem. The stripe matched the color of his aged hair. As he moved into the chamber, his old sullen eyes scanned the items floating on the floor. Tears of anguish flowed down his cheeks, but when he saw Farmer, he ran to her, smiling in recognition. The two villagers embraced; they were the lone survivors of the disaster. When they finally separated, Crafter stepped forward.

"Cobbler, this is Crafter," Farmer explained. "He has accepted me into his village. I am no longer one of the Lost."

"And we gladly accept you into our community," Crafter added. "You need not be alone anymore."

Cobbler looked down at the young NPC and smiled, his tears changing to that of joy instead of pain.

"Please tell us what happened here," Gameknight asked.

The NPC looked at the letters over Gameknight's head, then glanced up into the air, looking for the server thread that was not there. Cobbler's mouth hung open in shock as he realized who was standing before him.

"Yeah, yeah, he's the User-that-is-not-a-user. Get over it," Hunter said. "We need to know what happened here."

Monkeypants271 moved forward and stood next to Hunter's side. He put a calming hand on her shoulder.

"Our friend here has had a difficult time," Monkeypants said. "We need to have a little patience."

Cobbler looked at Monkeypants and noticed the letters above his head and the lack of a server thread.

"Yeah, and there's two of them, but we don't have time to be patient," Hunter said. "Cobbler, we need to know what happened here."

The NPC glanced around at all the armored villagers in the chamber, then leaned against the cavern wall and dropped his face into his hands. His body shook as he wept. Farmer put her arms around the NPC as she, too, cried. Slowly, the friends separated, wiping tears from their cheeks. Cobbler then brought his gaze to Crafter.

"I'm sure Farmer told you what happened here," Cobbler began. "Endermen and the Ender Dragon did this terrible thing. They destroyed everyone without hesitation, and for only one reason."

"A reason?" Farmer said, surprised. "What reason could there possibly be for all this destruction?"

Cobbler looked at his friend and sighed.

"They wanted to deliver a message to him," Cobbler said, pointing an old gnarled finger at Gameknight999.

"They destroyed all these lives just to deliver a message to me?" Gameknight asked.

Cobbler nodded his gray head.

"What message?" the User-that-is-not-a-user growled through clenched teeth. He was infuriated and ashamed.

"One of the endermen was different than the rest," Cobbler began. "He was colored a dark red instead of black."

"Feyd, the king of the endermen," Digger said, an angry scowl on his face. "I hoped we'd seen the last of that monster."

"What did he do?" Crafter asked.

Cobbler sighed again, then closed his eyes as the memories flooded through him.

"They came into the crafting chamber like a purple fog. The endermen just teleported right up to us, their purple teleportation particles filling the air. Something up above must have enraged them because they didn't wait to be provoked down here, they just attacked." Cobbler stopped, opened his eyes, and looked at Farmer, new cube-shaped tears sliding down his cheeks. "They first destroyed all the minecarts, but only after they let a few escape, then they turned on the remaining NPCs. The monsters didn't care if their targets were adults or children, they just attacked . . . and destroyed."

"But how did you survive?" Crafter asked.

"The red one grabbed me with one of his clammy hands and pinned me against the wall," Cobbler said. "He told me, 'You will watch and report what happens here to my enemy.' He then said, 'I want the User-that-is-not-a-user to know that his ancient foe has returned and is coming for him. There is no place he can hide,' and then he said something about punishing you for crimes committed against the monsters of Minecraft." The NPC stopped for a moment as he was overcome with emotion, then continued. "I was so afraid, I couldn't fight back. I wanted to do something, but I was petrified and couldn't even move my arms."

"It's OK, friend," Crafter said. "This was not your fault."

"No, this is *my* fault," Gameknight snapped. "I should have killed that monster when I had the chance, and now look what has happened."

"That enderman isn't finished," Cobbler continued. "He said something about destroying the next closest village when they find it."

"What?!" Gameknight exclaimed. "We have to get there first and warn them. Crafter, do you know how to get there in the minecarts?"

"Of course," the young NPC said.

"Then let's go!" Gameknight commanded. "Farmer, Cobbler, take the horses and go back to our village. The wolves will protect you." He glanced to Herder. The skinny boy nodded his head, then bolted up to the surface to give the commands to the pack leader. "The rest of you, we have to get to that village before it's too late!"

Crafter pulled out stacks of iron ingots and handed them out, then moved to the crafting benches. They crafted minecarts quickly. When they had finished, a dozen carts were ready, one for everyone. Gameknight took his and placed it on the track behind Crafter. He climbed in, drew his diamond sword with his right hand and his iron sword with his left.

"Let's do this!" Gameknight shouted to his comrades and followed Crafter into the darkness.

CHAPTER 7
ENEMY REVEALED

Gameknight999 leapt out of the minecart and into the new crafting chamber when the minecart emerged from the tunnel. His heart sank as he saw the items strewn about on the rocky cavern floor.

They were too late. The endermen had already wreaked terrible destruction on this village too. Not waiting for anyone else, Gameknight charged up the sandstone steps that led to the surface.

"Gameknight, wait for the others!" Crafter shouted, but he was ignored.

Gameknight pushed open the iron doors and bolted through the round chamber, sprinting through the tunnel that would take him to the vertical ladder that led to the surface above. As he ran, he could hear footsteps echoing behind him. Turning, he readied himself for battle. Instead, Stitcher emerged from the darkness with no intention of slowing down to talk.

"Come on, let's go," she said, streaking past him.

He followed. More footsteps sounded behind him, but he ignored them and kept running, thinking

only about getting to the surface and saving someone . . . anyone. He scaled the tall ladder as fast as
he could. When he reached the top, he saw Stitcher's lithe form climbing the ladders that would take
her to the topmost level of the watchtower.

Leaping high into the air, he grabbed the third
rung and climbed after her. In seconds, he was at
the top. All around the watchtower, he could now
see many items dispersed throughout the village,
tools discarded and food left to decay in the sun.
Every single villager was gone, destroyed by Feyd
and his army of monsters.

Gameknight growled.

"We're too late!" he snapped.

"But just barely," Stitcher said as she pointed
out across the desert dunes.

In the distance, Gameknight999 could see the
army of endermen moving away from the village,
the dragon flying high in the air, carving out lazy
circles above the dark nightmares. He could just
barely make out a dark red enderman at the head
of the formation: Feyd.

Drawing his sword, Gameknight turned toward
the ladder, but Stitcher's hand grabbed the back of
his armor.

"Don't be foolish," she said. "There are too many
of them and too few of us. It would be suicide."

Gameknight turned his head and glared at his
friend, but she was right. Sheathing his sword, he
moved back to the tower's edge and stared out at
the enemy forces. Below, he could hear his friends
moving out into the village, looking fruitlessly for
survivors.

Just then, he saw the dragon turn to look back
at the village.

"Quick, HIDE!" Gameknight shouted.

Gameknight crouched behind one of the stone crenellations that ringed the tower's peak. Stitcher had done the same, hiding behind a stone cube. Slowly, as the time passed, a strange feeling tickled in the back of his mind. The tickle turned to an itch . . . and then a burn. Somehow, Gameknight could feel the dragon's emotions through the fabric of Minecraft. He didn't understand it, but he could somehow sense the monster's vicious hatred in the distance . . . and there was something familiar there, something he'd felt before.

Chancing a glance, Gameknight edged his head around the sandstone and peeked around the block's edge. In the hazy distance, the User-that-is-not-a-user could see the dragon hovering in the air, staring back at the village. It was surrounded by sparkling purple and sickly yellow particles; they gave the monster a sinister and diseased look. Gameknight expected to see purple eyes staring back at him, but to his surprise he saw two intense white rectangles, blazing with the hatred of a thousand suffering lives.

And at that moment, Gameknight recognized his enemy—Herobrine.

Somehow the terrible virus had survived the void and had infected the Ender Dragon. *How is this possible?* he thought. Gameknight pulled his head back and sat on the ground against the stone block, his mind reeling.

"Gameknight, what's wrong?" Stitcher asked. "You're as pale as a ghast."

"Look at the eyes of the dragon, but be careful it doesn't see you."

Stitcher leaned out just enough to move one eye past the block. A gasp escaped her mouth as she pulled back and sat down, her face as white as Gameknight's.

"It can't be," she whispered, not wanting the distant dragon to hear her. "It's Herobrine."

Gameknight nodded his head.

"But how can that be?" she asked.

He shook his head as thoughts exploded in his mind.

We threw him into the void, he thought. *I saw him fall . . . saw his terrible eyes blink and go out. How can he still be alive?*

Memories of every battle with that terrible virus played through his mind as he sat there, shaking with fear.

How am I going to stop him now? He's a dragon!

Sneaking another glance around the block of stone, Gameknight could see Herobrine turn and fly back toward his army of endermen, a mist of purple and pale yellow particles still surrounding the giant.

Suddenly, a monkey's head popped up through the hole in the floor with a worried look on the face.

"You two OK up here?" Monkeypants asked.

Neither of them answered. They just shook their heads, fear in their eyes. Monkeypants glanced up at his son.

"What is it?" he asked.

"Herobrine . . . he's back," Gameknight mumbled.

"How's that possible?" his father asked.

"I don't know, but we need to get out of here," Gameknight said. "He might have seen us."

Glancing around the block one more time, he looked across the landscape. The army of dark monsters had moved farther away, their shadowy forms disappearing in the haze. He stood, motioned for his father to move down the ladder, and then followed him. At the foot of the watchtower, he found the rest of their party gathered together, looks of despair on their faces as they surveyed the now useless items that littered the village.

"I know who the enemy is," Gameknight said as he moved next to Crafter.

"Of course—it's that terrible endermen king, Feyd," Hunter said.

Gameknight shook his head.

"No," the User-that-is-not-a-user said. "That's what I thought, but my ancient enemy is not Feyd. It is someone much worse."

"Worse than an enderman," Hunter said. "What could possibly be worse than Feyd, the king of the endermen?"

"His master and maker . . . Herobrine," Gameknight said in a low voice.

"Herobrine? That can't be right," Digger said. "We all saw him fall into the void. He can't still be alive."

"We saw him from the top of the watchtower," Stitcher added. "I saw his eyes. I know it's him. He's back."

"I have no doubt it's him," Gameknight continued. "We all heard the music of Minecraft. Only one thing could hurt the Oracle and make the music sound that wounded—Herobrine."

"But how could he have been reborn into the form of the dragon?" Crafter asked.

"I don't know," the User-that-is-not-a-user answered. "Maybe his viral computer code infected the void and the dragon's egg. We all saw the egg on top of the exit portal when we left The End."

"It doesn't really matter how it happened," Crafter said. "All that's important is that Herobrine is back and we have to figure out what to do."

"What do you think we should do?" Digger asked, his deep booming voice filling the air.

"I don't know," Crafter replied. "I think I need to talk with the Council of Crafters and let them know what's going on. We must get back to our village as soon as possible."

The young NPC turned and headed back into the watchtower.

"What about all the items on the ground?" Herder asked.

"We should leave them as we did in Farmer's village," Crafter replied as he turned to look at the young boy.

"No!" Gameknight snapped. "We will need every-thing we can find to stop Herobrine and his mon-sters. Who knows how many creatures he really has in his army? Everyone, go and collect all the items."

No one moved; they just stared back at Game-knight. Ignoring their looks, he turned and moved throughout the village, collecting tools and food and weapons.

"Come on!" he shouted. "This isn't going to be as easy as all the other battles we've faced with Herobrine."

"The others were easy?" Hunter asked.

"Before, he was just a person like you and me," Gameknight said as he stopped and turned to face the others. "Now he's a dragon and has all the strength of that flying beast, but likely he still has his own powers as well. He might very well be impossible to defeat now. We need everything we can find to help." He took a step toward the others and glared at them. "I know you don't want to take these items, and I don't feel good about it either, but if we don't use everything we have to stop Herobrine, he may win. Isn't it more important to stop him from hurting other villagers? Wouldn't the villagers who lost their lives today have wanted us to do everything we could to keep other villages from suffering the same fate?"

They nodded their heads.

"Then get out here and help me collect all these items."

Still, the NPCs didn't move. Finally Monkeypants-271 stepped forward. As he passed Stitcher, he grabbed her small hand and pulled her with him. The pair nodded at Gameknight999 and then split up and collected items along the shattered wall. Following their example, the rest of the NPCs moved out into the village and picked up all of the discarded items. Going into the homes, they searched chests and furnaces, taking anything that might be helpful. When they had scoured the village clean, the party went back to the crafting chamber.

Following Crafter, they each took a minecart and jumped on the track that would lead them home. Gameknight and Monkeypants were the last to leave.

"Are you OK?" Monkeypants asked his son.

"I don't know, Dad," he answered. "I'm not sure I can do this. Herobrine? As the Ender Dragon? It can't get any worse than that." He then lowered his voice, even though they were alone. "I'm afraid I might fail my friends this time, and that fear is overpowering. It's making it difficult to think about what to do . . . difficult to try to help my friends."

Gameknight looked at the ground, ashamed at what he was feeling.

"Son, we have an obligation to help our friends whenever we can, not because we must, but because we choose to. The only thing worse than not helping someone in need is quitting when it becomes too hard." His father paused for a moment to let those words sink in. "A famous general once said, 'Age wrinkles the body. Quitting wrinkles the soul.' If you don't do everything you can possibly do to help your friends, you will regret it the rest of your life."

Gameknight999 looked up at his father.

"I know that you can solve this puzzle and help your friends," Monkeypants said. "All we need is for *you* to be as confident about it as I am. Now let's get back to the village and get this done."

Slapping his son on the back, his father jumped into his minecart and shot down the tracks into the darkness. Lifting his own minecart, Gameknight placed it on the tracks and climbed in, but looked back at the empty crafting chamber. At one time, it had been filled with life, and now it only held silence.

Was that the fate for all of Minecraft?

Gameknight shuddered as fear rippled down his spine. Shaking his body as though he were trying to dislodge the sensation, the User-that-is-not-a-user pushed his minecart into the darkness.

CHAPTER 8

THE ZOMBIE KING

Feyd materialized in the rocky tunnel. It was lit with an orange glow and smoke and ash filled the air. Off to the left, a column of lava fell from high up on the wall. The molten flow splashed when it hit the ground, creating a wide boiling pool. The temperature in the tunnel was hot and delicious. To the right, a stream of water spilled from a gap in the ceiling. The cool blue liquid ran down the sloping floor until it sizzled into the boiling stone. Where the two met, dark shining obsidian was formed.

This was the place.

Looking at a flat section of the tunnel wall, Feyd could see a single block of stone that stuck out. The area around the lone cube was flat and smooth. Teleporting to the stone, the enderman reached up and pressed the block. It moved ever so slightly, then clicked into place, causing internal mechanisms to move. The sound of stone grinding against stone filled the passage as a large section of the wall moved aside, revealing a long, dark tunnel. At the other end of the shadowy corridor, the endermen king could see the sparkling green light of a zombie HP fountain.

Gathering his teleportation powers, Feyd moved to the other end of the tunnel at the speed of thought. When the teleportation particles cleared, the monster looked down on a massive cavern bigger than anything that could naturally occur. All across the floor of the cavern, small homes built out of every kind of material in Minecraft were strewn about in a random order. It was a like a complicated patchwork of colors and shapes, with each house different in shape and size from its neighbor.

To Feyd, it looked terrible. Why would these creatures need to live in houses when they were already in a perfectly good cave? He never really understood these decaying monsters.

In the past, endermen used to bring blocks they stole from the NPCs into these zombie-towns. Their green brothers would use them to build. However their sharing had been cut back since the failure to capture the User-that-is-not-a-user in The End. Tensions were high between the zombies and the endermen, and Feyd was here to mend that rift and enlist the help of these creatures.

At the center of the massive cavern, Feyd saw a clearing—an area free of buildings, wide enough to allow a hundred zombies to congregate. A platform of obsidian sat at the center of the clearing; clearly this was a gathering center for the green monsters. Closing his eyes, he disappeared, then reappeared atop the dais, his presence still undetected.

These zombies really are fools, he thought.

Feyd looked about the clearing. The idiotic creatures shuffled about, doing whatever zombies do in zombie-town. Many were standing within the emerald flows of the HP fountains, rejuvenating themselves under the cascading green sparks. The fountains were placed throughout the cavern and kept the zombies tethered to their town; if they stayed on the surface of the Overworld too long, they would die. The fountains, like the endermen's need to teleport in The End, kept the monsters close to their designated homes and out of the Overworld. It was their punishment for past crimes against the NPCs in the early days after the Awakening, during the Great Zombie Invasion.

Suddenly, the sound of a sword smashing against a chest plate came from the direction of the patchwork hovels. Feyd knew this to be their alarm and a signal to gather in the central clearing; he'd have company soon. The sound caused the monsters to move faster, and those in rapturous delight under the emerald fountains snapped into action. In seconds, the clearing filled with zombies, their green bodies pressing in toward the raised obsidian platform. Quickly, they surrounded the king of the endermen, but stayed at least four blocks from the dark creature; none of them wanted to be within arm's reach.

As they looked up at him, moaning, Feyd could hear the sound of jingling metal from behind. When he turned, he found the hulking form of Xa-Tul approaching, his chainmail swaying on this body as he pushed through the green decaying creatures. The light from the numerous HP fountains bounced off the metallic links, casting a shower of green reflections on the monsters around him, giving the appearance that the hulking monster wore a coat of rare emeralds. Nearing the dark platform, the zombie king drew his huge golden broadsword and pointed it at the enderman.

"What does an enderman want here in zombie-town?" Xa-Tul boomed.

"I have come to talk," Feyd replied in a screechy voice. "Why don't you put your little sword away before someone gets hurt?"

"Xa-Tul will put it away when Xa-Tul chooses," the zombie king replied. "The endermen left the zombies in The End for too long. Many were close to death when they were returned to zombie-town. The endermen king did that on purpose to punish us for something that was not our fault."

"They had the Maker with them," Feyd screeched. "If your zombies had stopped the User-that-is-not-a-user in the stronghold, then Herobrine could have been saved right then."

"Xa-Tul did not know the pathetic NPCs had the Maker with them!" the zombie complained. "Nor did the endermen know this. This failure belonged more to the endermen than it did the zombies."

The monsters around the dark platform growled and moaned as they listened to the debate. Some of them stepped closer, their razor sharp claws slowly extending from stubby fingertips.

"I am not here to relive this argument, Xa-Tul," Feyd explained. "I am here to deliver orders."

"Orders!" the monster scoffed. "Xa-Tul does not take orders from an enderman."

"They are not my orders. They are the Maker's."

Xa-Tul laughed.

"Xa-Tul knows the Maker was thrown into the void," the zombie king explained. "And Feyd knows it as well. The Maker is dead."

The zombie king raised his clawed hand high up into the air, fingers spread wide, then clenched it into a fist as he moaned sorrowfully, the rest of the zombies doing the same.

"The salute of sacrifice is given for the Maker," Xa-Tul said.

"For the clan!" shouted some of the other monsters.

"For the clan!"

"For the clan!"

Feyd waited impatiently for the monsters to finish, then glared down at Xa-Tul, his eyes glowing dangerously white.

"You fool, the Maker is not dead—he still lives!"

"What?" Xa-Tul asked. "Feyd says that Herobrine still lives. Is this a joke?"

"Herobrine does not joke, nor do I," the king of the endermen screeched. "He has commanded me to bring the zombie nation into his new war. You are ordered to—"

"Zombies no longer take orders from endermen," Xa-Tul growled. "That has happened in the past and it will not happen ever again. Feyd says that Herobrine is still alive yet no proof is offered. How can this be possible after the Maker was thrown into the void? Why should the zombies believe this?"

"Herobrine came back in the form of the Ender Dragon," Feyd explained.

Xa-Tul laughed, then turned and looked at the zombies around him. The decaying creatures gave a growling, moaning sort of laugh at the sound of this explanation.

"How is that possible?" Xa-Tul asked. "Does the king of the endermen think that zombies are fools? Nothing survives the void; every creature in Minecraft knows this."

"The Maker has powers beyond anything we understand, for he was able to infect the dragon's egg and be reborn." Feyd took a step to the edge of the platform and glared down at the zombie king. "I am done arguing with you. Herobrine commands that you bring your zombies to him at once. Any delay will be dealt with swiftly and with a lethal response." Feyd leaned closer to the zombie king. "What is your reply?"

Xa-Tul smiled up at the enderman king, his sharp pointed zombie-teeth shining in the green light of the HP fountains.

"Xa-Tul doesn't like the king of the endermen and does not trust him," the zombie king growled. "The zombies will not listen to these childish stories and be made to look like fools. Be gone from zombie-town and never return. Feyd is no longer welcome here." Xa-Tul then raised his voice so that all could hear, the tone changing from an explanation to that of a command. "If Feyd ever returns to our home, the zombies will protect themselves and fall on the king of the endermen as though he were an invader. Leave, now, while you still can!"

"So you refuse?" Feyd asked, a wry smile showing on his face. "Good. I will enjoy watching when the Maker comes here himself. He will not be happy."

"Be gone, enderman, and take your pathetic stories with you," Xa-Tul moaned.

Glaring at the zombies nearest the obsidian platform, he motioned them to advance. With a growl, the zombies climbed up onto the dais and approached the enderman, arms extended and claws glistening.

Glancing about him, Feyd saw the monsters closing in. With eyes flaring bright white, he disappeared and teleported to the cavern entrance before any of them could get close. He glared down on the collection of fools, his eyes blazing with anger.

"You have made your choice, Xa-Tul, and have chosen your fate," Feyd screeched. "Now it is up to the Maker to choose your punishment. Enjoy the consequences of your decision!"

The king of the endermen let out a wicked cackle, then disappeared in a cloud of purple mist.

CHAPTER 9

THE COUNCIL OF CRAFTERS

Gameknight emerged from the tunnel and sighed. They were finally home, back in Crafter's village. Familiar people greeted him as he stepped out of the minecart and lifted the metallic vehicle off the tracks. After placing it in a nearby chest, Gameknight scanned the sea of faces for Crafter. He found him inspecting a pile of swords built by some of the workers in the crafting chamber. Carefully testing the edge of the blades with his blocky thumb, the young NPC nodded as he placed the iron sword back in the pile, the NPCs nearby beaming with pride. Weaving his way around crafting benches and minecart rails, Gameknight moved to his friend's side.

"Everyone looks busy," he said.

"They've been working hard while we were gone," Crafter said. "They all heard the strained music and know something is going on; they just don't know what it is . . . yet."

"Perhaps we should keep the details of . . . you know who . . . and his dark friends to ourselves until after we talk to the other crafters," Gameknight suggested in a low voice.

Crafter nodded, his blond hair falling into his face and covering one of his bright blue eyes.

Off to the side of the chamber, Gameknight could see his father talking to some of the workers. With his sword, the monkey sketched something on the ground and the NPC workers nodded their understanding. Curious, Gameknight crossed the chamber and tapped his father on the arm. As he turned to face his son, the workers moved off, heading up the steps and to the village.

"What are you doing?" the User-that-is-not-a-user asked.

"Just giving the workers something to do," Monkeypants replied, a guilty look on his face.

What are you up to, Dad? he thought.

"Gameknight, Monkeypants—this way," Crafter said over the din of the crafting chamber.

Gameknight saw Crafter standing against a blank wall of stone, his pickaxe in his hand. Gameknight motioned for his father to follow and then moved through the busy cavern. Stepping over minecart tracks and curving around workers, the father and son snaked their way through the busy room until they stood next to the young NPC leader.

"I thought we needed to talk to the Council of Crafters?" Gameknight said.

"We do," Crafter replied.

Gameknight looked around the busy chamber. There was only one way in and one way out: the tall flight of steps that led to the tunnels and the surface. The User-that-is-not-a-user gave his friend a confused look.

"We have to go down near the bedrock level," Crafter replied, answering the unasked question.

"Bedrock level?" Monkeypants asked.

"When you dig down to the lowest levels of Minecraft, you find bedrock," Gameknight explained. "It's not possible to break through bedrock when you're in survival mode, so that's as far as you can go."

"What's on the other side of the bedrock?" his father asked.

"The void," Gameknight answered.

"Exactly," Crafter replied. "And it is through the void that we are able to communicate with the other crafters."

"What?" Gameknight asked.

Crafter ignored the question and swung his pickaxe. The sharp iron tip dug into the wall, sending sharp gray shards of stone flying in all directions. After three quick hits, the block disappeared, revealing a dark passageway. Crafter smashed a second box and created a small opening. Looking over the young NPC's shoulder, Gameknight could see a long stairway that plunged down into the flesh of Minecraft. Torches were placed economically along the sidewall, creating small circles of light amidst the darkness.

"The council chamber is down here," Crafter said, running down the steps without hesitation. Gameknight gave his father a questioning glance, then followed his friend, Monkeypants just a step behind. As they descended, he tried to count the number of stairs, but quickly lost track. He knew the crafting chamber was maybe twenty blocks below the surface of the village, so the bedrock would likely be another hundred blocks beneath that.

Descending from one circle of torchlight to the next, Gameknight thought about all those NPCs that had perished at the hand, or claw, of Herobrine and his army of endermen. How was he going to battle Herobrine, now that the terrible virus was in dragon form? It was hard enough just battling Herobrine, or the dragon, but combined? It was impossible.

I just want to run away and hide, Gameknight thought. *I know I can't do that to my friends, though—they need me. But what if I fail and get some of them hurt, or worse?*

Waves of uncertainty and fear flooded through his mind as he followed the distant form of Crafter. He was tempted many times to stop and retreat, but Gameknight could hear his father's steps right behind him. Surprisingly, the thought of his dad being right there pushed back a little on the shadowy specters of fear that prowled his mind. His dad's confidence and positive outlook was shockingly comforting.

Maybe with his father's help, he could . . .

Suddenly, they were there. Before him sat a chamber lit with a single torch. It was only three blocks high, but stretched out in all directions beyond the circle of illumination cast by the flickering light. The ground was covered with cold, striped blocks of black and gray, their appearance almost dizzying as they stretched out into the darkness.

Near the staircase, Gameknight could see a 3-by-3 grid of diamond blocks. Sitting atop the center block was a beacon, but it was dark and silent. No light streamed from the glassy block. Its interior was a cool glacial blue.

"What is that?" Monkeypants asked.

"It's a beacon," Gameknight replied. "It can send a beam of light high into the air and give you special capabilities when you are near. But right now it's not active."

"It doesn't look like it is doing anything," his father commented.

"That's right, it's not," Crafter replied. "It needs clear air directly above it, and there is a block up there covering it up."

"Do we need to go up and break it away?" Gameknight asked.

Crafter shook his head. Reaching to the ground behind the diamond blocks, Gameknight could see the young NPC flip a lever. Instantly a line of redstone powder lit up and turned bright red. The trail of red dust led across the bedrock until it ended at a stack of cobblestone. But instead of it being a continuous stack of stone, a redstone torch sat between each pair of blocks: a redstone ladder. As soon as the signal reached the first block, the redstone torches activated. Every other one lit up and glowed red, while the others stayed dark. This allowed the signal to traverse vertically up to some kind of mechanism. Gameknight heard a piston move somewhere far away, the sound barely audible through the redstone ladder.

Suddenly, the beacon came to life and a shaft of brilliant white light shot up into the air. The glow from the beam lit the bedrock chamber, pushing back the shadows in all directions. Looking about him, Gameknight could now see that the cavern extended out as far as the render distance would allow.

Gameknight noticed the beam was actually a square shaft of light that appeared to be slowly rotating about its center. The middle of the beam looked almost solid, but when Gameknight moved his hand through the intense light, he felt it tingle.

The beacon was humming and crackling as though it were alived. It reminded Gameknight of an angry hive of bees or an old static-filled radio. It almost reminded him of the digitizer that first time he'd been accidently transported into Minecraft.

"That's a beacon?" Monkeypants asked, his eyes wide with excitement. He was transfixed, his face filled with wonder at the beautiful display of light.

"Yep, that's a beacon," Gameknight said, nodding his head.

"Down here, near the void, it lets us communicate with the other server planes," Crafter added. "The other beacons will start to hum, telling their crafters to activate their own beacons. In no time, we will be able to talk with them. But remember—"

Suddenly, a crackling sound erupted from the shaft of light as another humming sound could be heard. But the new humming was a different note than their beacon. The two sounds harmonizing together.

"Ahh, someone has already joined," Crafter said with a smile, then leaned toward Gameknight999. "Please be quiet and listen. The Council of Crafters can only be attended by full crafters, so you must remain silent."

Gameknight and Monkeypants both nodded their heads.

Moving up next to the beacon, the young NPC placed three blocks of wool on the ground, then sat on one. He pointed at Gameknight and Monkeypants and gestured to the soft cubes. The father and son sat down and stared at the beautiful shaft of light. In minutes, they could hear multiple tones humming from the beacon, the entire ensemble sounding like an orchestra of bees, each buzzing their own instrument in a fantastic, harmonious symphony.

"Are we all here?" Crafter asked.

Buzzing voices floated from the shaft of light, each one affirming their presence.

"We are all here, Crafter," one of the voices said. "Why have you called this unexpected meeting of the council?"

"Our ancient foe still lives and threatens Minecraft," Crafter said as he leaned forward and spoke into the beacon like it was a microphone.

"How can this be?" one of the voices hummed. "You cast him into the void. The evil lights in his eyes extinguished—you saw this yourself. Now you say he is back . . . inconceivable."

"There is much we do not understand about the void," Crafter said. "Perhaps it is only deadly to creatures of the Overworld and not—"

"We know it is deadly to *all* creatures," snapped a lower tone from the shaft of light. "If you threw him in, then he is gone and you must be mistaken."

"He cannot have survived," another voice said, "unless you were mistaken about Herobrine falling into the emptiness."

"No, I am not mistaken!" Crafter snapped. "It must have happened because—"

"It doesn't matter how it happened!" Gameknight shouted. Getting up from the wool, he stood right in front of the shaft of light. He could feel his heart pump faster, as though he were sprinting. He felt his legs strengthen, as if they could propel him much higher up into the air. "Listen to me, Herobrine is back in the Overworld, but in the form of the Ender Dragon. He is leading an army of endermen and—"

Like the buzzing of an angry hive, the voices of the other crafters all came across the beacon at the same time. They argued and shouted, some believing this was the end of Minecraft, while others claimed that it was a lie.

"Wait a minute, everyone be quiet," one voice said, the sound of command filling their voice. The other crafters became silent. "Who is this talking?"

"This is Gameknight999, the User-that-is-not-a-user," he shouted with pride, "and I have seen the Herobrine-dragon with my own eyes."

"A user?!" the crafters exclaimed. "The beacons are only for crafters. Crafter, what have you done? You have transgressed the law."

"No, I haven't," Crafter replied. "The law states that the beacons are for crafters and not for NPCs. Gameknight999 and his father are not NPCs."

"His father is there, too?!" someone else yelled.

"You crafters need to focus on what is important," Gameknight said, his voice stern, as if he were lecturing a small child. "Herobrine is wiping out village after village as he moves across Minecraft. I don't think he will stop until he destroys everything. Since he obviously still has his teleportation powers, when he finishes with this server, he will go to the next one and the next one until all of the server planes are wiped clean."

"He must be stopped!" shouted one crafter.

"It cannot be allowed!" said another.

"No, we can't let him . . ."

"It isn't right, we will . . ."

"Stand and fight with . . ."

All of the crafters spoke at once until the leader finally quelled the confusion.

"Brothers," the leader said. "This is dire news. Herobrine must be stopped. The User-that-is-not-a-user is correct: if Herobrine isn't stopped on that server, then he will eventually destroy everything. At that point, the pyramid of server plains will destabilize and all of it will come crashing down, giving him access to the Source. He must be stopped."

Crafter sighed. Gameknight could see a look of resignation on his friend's face. Gameknight knew his friend had an idea, and was dreading voicing it. Crafter sighed again.

"I know what must be done," Crafter said.

The voices on the other side of the beacons became silent.

"Herobrine cannot be allowed to leave this server plane," Crafter explained. "We will try to stop him, but if we cannot, then this plane must be disconnected from the Source."

A gasp came from the beam, the buzzing voices clearly in shock at what was just said.

"Crafter is right," the commanding voice said. "If they cannot stop the enemy, and he tries to teleport from that server, then it must be severed from the pyramid of servers and from the Source. Is it agreed?"

Murmurs of affirmation buzzed from the shaft of light, but with each confirmation, Crafter's face became more determined . . . and scared.

"The vote is complete. We will do as Crafter suggests," the leader explained. "Crafter, do what you must. User-that-is-not-a-user, we need you now more than ever. Please help us, for the lives of everyone on all the server planes rests in your hands."

The voices then silenced as the harmonious buzzing from the beacon slowly disappeared, leaving just its shaft of light. Reaching to the lever, Crafter turned off the redstone circuit, causing the piston high overhead to move back into place, blocking the beam and extinguishing the beacon.

Bathed in just the torchlight of the bedrock chamber, Gameknight could see the look of worry on his friend's face.

"Crafter, what did they mean, 'Sever it from the pyramid'?" Gameknight asked.

Crafter stood and turned to look at the father and son. Eerie shadows stretched across his stern face as he picked up the block of cotton and put it back into his inventory.

"Crafter . . . what is it?" Gameknight asked again.

His friend took a deep breath and blew it out slowly, fear and uncertainty filling his bright blue eyes.

"We cannot allow Herobrine to take his campaign of destruction across the server planes," the young NPC explained. "If that happens, he could destabilize everything. He has to be stopped on this server, at any cost."

"Of course. We're going to do everything we can to stop him," Gameknight affirmed. "We aren't going to stop trying until we are successful."

"Yes, I know," Crafter answered. "But if we cannot stop him, and it looks as if he is going to teleport to a new server plane, then the other crafters will have no choice but to disconnect us from the Source."

"How do they do that?" Monkeypants asked.

"You weren't at the Source," Crafter said. "But Gameknight was there. He knows what it looks like."

Gameknight nodded his head.

"Each world is connected to the Source through a beacon that looks like this one before you," Crafter continued. "The other crafters will watch our progress, and if it looks like we cannot stop Herobrine, then they will shatter the beacon that leads to our server, disconnecting us from the pyramid of server planes, and the Source."

"So what?" Gameknight asked. "That will give us more time to defeat Herobrine. He won't be able to escape."

Crafter turned and faced his friend, a look of grim resolution on his square face.

"You don't get it. If the crafters disconnect our server from the Source, then our server will crash and all computer code will be stopped." Crafter reached out and placed a hand on Gameknight's shoulder. "It will be the end of everything here."

"You mean you will . . ."

Crafter nodded his head. "All life on the server will cease. We will all die, including Herobrine. That is the weapon of last resort, but with Herobrine in the Ender Dragon's body, we can't take any chances. Better to sacrifice one world than lose them all."

Gameknight was stunned; he didn't know how to respond. This wasn't a solution. It was extermination!

This is too much, Gameknight thought. *If I can't stop Herobrine, then everyone on this server will die. How can I handle all that responsibility?*

A hand settled on his shoulder from behind. Turning, he saw his father looking at him, his big monkey eyes filled with confidence in his son.

"Responsibility is an opportunity to succeed, but only if you have faith in yourself," Monkeypants said.

"But the dragon is so big and strong. We can't destroy it when it's—"

"Don't focus on what you *can't* do," his father said. "Always plan for success. Focus on what you *can* do, and then get it done. Giving up isn't an option."

Gameknight looked to the ground, ashamed that he was thinking that very thought.

"You aren't going to quit and you know it, so stop considering it," Monkeypants said. "As I've taught you many times, break down the problem into smaller pieces, and attack the pieces. When all the pieces have been vanquished, then the problem is solved." Monkeypants took a step closer to his son and stared down at him. "Now, what's the first small problem that concerns you about Herobrine?"

Gameknight thought for a moment and then looked up into his father's eyes. "We don't know where he is or where he is going."

"That sounds like a solvable problem," Monkeypants said.

Gameknight looked at Crafter and then back to his father, a small smile on his face as plans within plans started circulating in his mind.

CHAPTER 10

HEROBRINE IN ZOMBIE-TOWN

Herobrine soared high overhead, gazing down at his endermen army. From this height, they looked like tiny black dots against the snow-covered landscape. They'd passed from the wonderful savannah plains to this cursed frozen river biome. Though the layer of ice that sat atop the river did not hurt the dark endermen, the deadly water that flowed beneath still terrified the creatures.

He knew their tiny black feet found little traction on the frozen surface, causing them to slip and fall as they walked awkwardly across the river. They could have easily teleported across the landscape, but Herobrine had instructed the monsters to conserve their strength for the next battle. While a small handful of scouts were teleporting across the landscape, looking for the next village, the remainder of his forces walked through the biome, hoping to stumble onto the next community of NPCs.

Overwhelming hatred filled Herobrine's mind as he thought about what he'd seen at the last village. Just as they had been leaving the destroyed settlement, he had experienced a strange, familiar feeling—something he'd picked up through the fabric of Minecraft. When he looked back at the village, he swore he'd seen his adversary, Gameknight999, hiding atop the watchtower.

"I'm sure it was you, my enemy," he said to the empty air, his eyes glowing bright.

He wasn't sure how, but he knew what he saw and knew what he felt: it had been the User-that-is-not-a-user. However, he knew attacking him then would have been dangerous. Herobrine had underestimated the User-that-is-not-a-user too many times, and that annoying Gameknight999 always seemed to have some trick up his sleeve. No, this time, Herobrine would make sure he had overwhelming numbers on his side, and this small collection of endermen was not enough to ensure victory.

Letting his anger dissipate, the dragon descended to watch as his troops crossed a wide section of ice. Suddenly, Herobrine heard ice breaking accompanied by a pain-filled screech. Turning his gaze toward the sound, he could see one of his endermen had fallen through the ice. Flashing red as soon as the monster splashed into the chilly waters, it immediately teleported to safety. Tendrils of smoke rose from the wet monster as it moved across a snow-covered hill, trying to get the water that still clung to its skin to evaporate and stop burning his flesh.

Another block of ice shattered, then another . . . and another. More shrieks of pain filled the air as the drenched endermen flashed red, then teleported to safety. The other monsters, seeing their comrades' pain, all teleported off the frozen river to the safety of the snow-frosted ground. As Herobrine watched the scene from overhead, he noticed movement from the distant edge of the river. Swooping down, he saw a form take shape: it looked like an NPC, but this one was clothed in glacial blues and snowy whites.

It was a light-crafter.

Herobrine roared as he dove toward his enemy.

Light-crafters were creatures created by the Oracle to offset the workings of his own shadow-crafters. By the looks of the pathetic little creature's clothing, Herobrine guessed this one was an ice-crafter and likely the one responsible for the ice breaking beneath his soldiers' feet.

Roaring, the dragon flapped his mighty wings, then extended his claws and accelerated.

"I'm going to destroy you!" Herobrine screamed.

The light-crafter looked up at the approaching dragon in surprise, then stood and smiled. This infuriated Herobrine even more. Flapping his wings harder, he reached out with his talons, ready to enjoy the moment of this idiotic creature's destruction. But just before he could reach his prey, the light-crafter moved across the ice with lighting speed, streaking across the frozen surface as though on magical skates. Following the curve in the frozen river, the light-crafter quickly disappeared into the haze, his icy mocking laughter driving the dragon into a rage. Herobrine could have followed in pursuit, but didn't want to leave his troops unprotected. Instead he turned and flew back to his army, now gathered atop a snowy hill.

As he approached, he saw a dark red enderman materialize amidst the darker monsters; Feyd had returned.

Flapping his wings once more to gain a little speed, Herobrine extended his leathery arms and glided on the soft breeze, silently approaching his troops. Circling the hilltop, he waited for his troops to clear a place for him to land, then gracefully settled down on the snow-covered ground.

"Feyd, king of the endermen, how many of the zombies will join us in the next battle?" Herobrine asked.

Feyd took a step back and lowered his gaze to the ground.

"None . . . Master."

"WHAT?!" the dragon roared. The other endermen stepped back as Herobrine's eyes grew brighter and brighter. "What do you mean?"

"Xa-Tul does not believe that you are still alive," Feyd explained. "He refused to send his troops to us."

"Did he now?" Herobrine sneered, his eyes glowing bright. "Endermen, I will be leaving you briefly. Get into defensive formations and watch out for our enemy, Gameknight999. Scouts, patrol the area."

Endermen zipped away, moving about the frozen landscape looking for threats as the bulk of the army formed a large circle, clenched fists and angry eyes pointing outward.

Satisfied, the dragon nodded his massive head, then turned his gaze toward his general.

"Take me to him—now!" the dragon commanded.

"Yes, Maker."

Feyd stepped forward and placed a hand on the dragon's massive paw. Instantly, they were both shrouded in a fog of purple particles. In a second, it cleared, revealing a huge cave, sparkling green HP fountains dotting the perimeter. Herobrine found he was standing atop an obsidian platform with zombies all around him. The green monsters were shuffling out of the clearing and back to their dilapidated homes. At the edge of the clearing was Xa-Tul, the big zombie king. Xa-Tul pushed his way through the smaller zombies, his chainmail swaying back and forth with each step.

Drawing in a deep breath, Herobrine let out a mighty roar that shook the cavern walls and knocked most of the zombies to the ground, save Xa-Tul. As the zombie king turned, Herobrine smiled and shot him a hateful glare, his eyes blazing bright white. Instantly, a look of fear came across Xa-Tul's face as he realized whom he was facing.

"All zombies, come forward and bow to the Maker!" Xa-Tul bellowed.

The zombies stood and stared in wonder at the Ender Dragon who sat on the central dais. Shuffling back into the clearing, the monsters looked up at Herobrine in reverence.

"Hurry and bow," Xa-Tul yelled. "Proper respect must be shown to Herobrine, the Maker."

"Ha!" laughed the dragon. "Proper respect? Is that what you showed my messenger, Feyd, when I ordered you to bring your zombie army to me?"

"Xa-Tul did not know that Herobrine still lived," the zombie king said. "The User-that-is-not-a-user dropped Herobrine into the void. It was impossible to survive."

"Yet here I am, standing before you again," Herobrine said. "If you want to survive, you should listen to my general, Feyd, instead of ignoring him. I have no use for disobedient commanders."

Xa-Tul took a step back. He reached for his sword, but as soon as his hand touched the hilt of his sword, the dragon leapt off the platform and landed amidst the zombies, his body surrounded by purple and pale yellow particles. Swinging his tail and slashing out with his talons, Herobrine destroyed a dozen zombies in the blink of an eye. When he was finished, he turned and moved toward Xa-Tul, stopping when he was face to face with the zombie king.

"You are still useful to me. That is the only reason why I allow you to live," Herobrine said. "But these zombies are nothing to me. I've destroyed them as a lesson to you and all zombies: follow my commands or be exterminated." He then leaned even closer to the zombie leader. "I need you to lead this rabble. Disobey me again and you won't even get a chance to reach for that pathetic sword of yours. Do you understand?"

Xa-Tul nodded his head and bowed low.

"Thank you, Maker, for the lesson," the zombie king said in a soft, respectful voice.

"Look up at me, you fool," Herobrine snapped.

Xa-Tul stood up straight and tall and looked into the dragon's blazing eyes.

"I have seen our enemy and he has seen me," Herobrine said.

"What?!" both Feyd and Xa-Tul exclaimed at the same time.

"He was in the last village. I saw him hiding atop the watchtower while we were leaving."

"We should have gone back and crushed him!" Feyd explained.

"All in good time, my Feyd," Herobrine said. "Destruction is an art form that must be done just right. We want the User-that-is-not-a-user to suffer before he is destroyed. It must be deliciously painful both physically and emotionally. That is why we will destroy *all* of his precious villages and

NPCs, letting him know along the way that he is responsible for their suffering. And when his despair is complete, I will force him to do my bidding and release me from the confines of these servers. And then revenge will truly begin!"

Herobrine released an evil, maniacal laugh, his eyes glaring bright, then moved back atop the obsidian platform. He addressed the zombies standing before him.

"Soon, we will find the next village and destroy it, not because we must, but because we *can*," Herobrine growled. "Zombies, you will lead the charge, with my endermen opening a pathway for you to move straight into the villages." The zombies started moaning excitedly. "Soon, you will be helping me to cleanse the surface of the Overworld and reclaim what was taken from you . . . the blue sky."

"The sky . . ."

"The sky . . ."

"The sky . . ."

Zombies murmured excitedly as they drew on the memories of their ancestors before being confined to the dark and lonely subterranean corners of the server. They all craved for that wide-open space over their heads instead of these rocky enclosures.

"Soon we will rule the Overworld and Minecraft will be ours!" Herobrine shouted. The dragon turned his large head toward the zombie king. "Be ready when I call, or meet your doom."

"The zombies *will* be ready," Xa-Tul promised.

"For your sake, I hope so," Herobrine replied.

Feyd then materialized next to the dragon and placed a hand on his dark paw. In a cloud of purple smoke, they disappeared, Herobrine's blazing white eyes the last thing to vanish from zombie-town.

CHAPTER 11

LOOKING FOR THE ENEMY

Riders went out on the minecart network, traveling to every village near the last site of destruction. Gameknight suspected that the endermen could not teleport infinite distances; there had to be some limit to their powers. As a result, they were more likely to find the village closest to the last one they'd destroyed.

While the riders searched, Crafter organized the warriors, gathering weapons, armor, food, and building materials for the upcoming battle. In the crafting chamber, NPCs banged out swords and chest plates as fast as their rectangular arms could work. Once they'd filled a cart with materials, they sent it down the minecart tracks to the village closest to the last attack.

"Crafter, we need to send the warriors to the next village," Gameknight said. "Are they ready?"

"We'll have to go up to the surface and check with Digger," Crafter replied. "He said that they—"

Suddenly, the iron doors at the top of the stairs burst open, and warriors in full armor streamed into the crafting chamber. Gameknight could see

Hunter and Stitcher at the front of the group, their bright red hair standing out against the sea of dull gray iron. In the middle of the group, Herder walked next to Digger's stocky form, and a handful of wolves followed obediently. When they reached the cavern floor, Herder moved off to the corner of chamber, his obedient pack behind him.

"Herder, you can't take your wolves with us to the next village," Gameknight said. "They won't go into the minecart."

"That's what I thought, too," the boy said. "I talked about it with Monkeypants. I told him every time I tried to get them to go into the cart, they refused."

"I'm not surprised," the User-that-is-not-a-user replied. "Then why are they here?"

"Well, your dad told me one of his rules."

"Oh no . . ." Gameknight muttered.

"Yeah," Herder replied, his voice filled with excitement. "He said 'Rule Number 2 is: when what you are doing doesn't work, try something else.' So I did. I tried something different and it worked!"

"What are you talking about?" Gameknight asked.

Herder moved to a minecart and the wolves followed close behind. Pulling out a leash, he connected it to a wolf's collar, then pulled the animal directly toward a cart. In an effort to get to its master, the wolf jumped into the cart, but before it could jump out, Herder moved forward and pushed it down the minecart track. The wolf disappeared into the darkness of the tunnel, its bark echoing off the tunnel walls.

The warriors in the chamber laughed, chanting "Wolfman! Wolfman! Wolfman!" He repeated the process over and over until a dozen wolves were on their way to the next village.

"Nice," Gameknight said, causing the young boy to beam with pride.

Without replying, Herder jumped into a mine-cart and moved down the tracks, following the pack of wolves.

"The rest of you get into a minecart," Digger boomed, his voice filling the chamber with the sound of command. "We need to get to the next village before the enemy arrives. Cavalry goes first, and as soon as they get to the village, they should find horses and scout the surrounding area. We must know where the monsters are. Now everyone, GO, GO, GO!"

The warriors piled into minecarts as fast as workers could put them on the tracks. It was like watching a river of iron as the armored NPCs shot down the dark tunnel. Gameknight knew the end of this tunnel was not their destination. They would have to travel through many more crafting chambers before they reached the village that Herobrine was likely to attack.

"Come on, Gameknight," Hunter said. "You don't want to miss any of the fun."

Before he could reply, she jumped into a minecart and disappeared into the darkness, with her younger sister, Stitcher, following close behind.

Suddenly, he sensed something behind him. Turning, Gameknight found the two light-crafters, Treebrin and Grassbrin, standing before him. The tall Treebrin towered over him, his dark tree bark–like skin standing out in contrast to Grassbrin's pale green skin.

"We are commming alongggg," Grassbrin said in his singsong voice.

"Grublator," grumbled Treebrin, his words always unrecognizable to Gameknight.

"Perhapssss we cannnn be of some help," the little green light-crafter said.

"Great, you are certainly welcome," Gameknight999 replied.

As the two light-crafters disappeared into the passage, Gameknight himself climbed into a cart and shot down the tunnel, his father following right behind. After moving through four crafting chambers, he finally reached the destination: the next village likely to be attacked.

Climbing out, Gameknight999 could see that all the other warriors had already moved up to the surface, using the secret tunnels that led to the cobblestone watchtower. As Gameknight emerged from the dark tunnels and stepped into the courtyard of the village, he was greeted by the sound of confusion and building. Climbing to the top of the watchtower, he looked about. A tall cobblestone wall surrounded the village, likely a remnant from the wave of destruction started by Erebus and Malacoda. Today it would be tested to its limit. Atop the wall, Gameknight could see tall archer towers being built. Digger was directing the workers to construct raised platforms so that an overlapping field of fire could be established. Outside of the wall, workers were burying blocks of TNT into the grassy plain and connecting pressure plates and tripwires to the explosive cubes. Hopefully their traps would go unnoticed until it was too late for the enemy.

Sadly, all these villagers knew exactly what to do to prepare for the fight of their lives. Ferocious monsters had hounded them since Gameknight had come into the game. It seemed a million years ago when he'd accidently triggered the digitizer, but now he was here of his own free will (and a little guilt), helping his friends fight off another threat to their existence.

"You look lost in thought," his father said as he approached.

"Just hoping we can help this village survive," Gameknight replied and then leaned closer. "Dad, you think we'll be enough to stop him?"

"I don't know," Monkeypants replied.

"Thanks, you're a big help," Gameknight scowled.

"In conflicts between nations, neither side is ever certain of the outcome," his father said. "But both feel so strongly about their cause that they are willing to go to war and do whatever they can to be successful. Do you believe in your cause?"

"Of course," Gameknight snapped. "Herobrine has terrorized the NPCs for too long. I'm sure he still wants to get out of the Minecraft servers and into the Internet so that he can seek vengeance on everyone in the physical world. He's insane and must be stopped."

"So it sounds to me like you believe in your cause and are willing to do your best to stop him."

"Of course. I won't let him hurt my friends," Gameknight said, his voice filled with conviction.

"Then just do what you gotta do to take care of this monster and don't give failure any thought. Worrying that you might fail is the first step to defeat. Do you understand?"

"I think so," Gameknight replied. "But what if I'm not—"

Before he could finish his statement, a shout came from outside the walls. Looking out from the watchtower, Gameknight could see a rider approaching. He was screaming as loud as he could, but was still too far away to be understood.

"What do you think he's saying?" Monkeypants asked.

"I don't know, but I bet it's not good news," Gameknight replied. "Come on, let's get to the gates."

Father and son slid down the ladder next to them and sprinted to the wooden gates, which stood open at the village entrance. Gameknight could see Crafter and Digger there with a handful of warriors at their sides. Most of the other NPCs had already taken up defensive positions on the walls and towers. As Gameknight reached Crafter's side, the rider approached, leaping off his gray mount when he was near.

"I saw them, a huge collection of endermen coming this way." The NPC had to stop to catch his breath for a moment. "There are maybe fifty or sixty of them in total, and there's a dragon flying high overhead."

"Only endermen. That's great. And fifty or sixty, that's not as bad as I thought," Digger said.

"Uh, did you hear the part about the dragon?" Hunter said as she approached.

Digger rolled his eyes. "We've killed a dragon before. This one is no different."

"Oh yeah?" Hunter replied, then turned to the horseman. "What color were the dragon's eyes?"

"Ahh, I think they were white," he replied. "That's kinda strange. You'd think they would be purple."

"That's because this is no ordinary dragon; it's Herobrine," Hunter said.

The horseman gasped, his rectangular eyes suddenly filled with fear.

"Hunter, we know who it is," Crafter said calmly. "But it doesn't matter. If he is threatening this village, then we are going to do everything we can to stop him. Now go up into your archer tower. We'll need your bow soon enough."

Giving them an exasperated grunt, she went back to the recently constructed tower on the edge of the wall.

"The dragon may be trouble," Crafter said, "but it sounds like Herobrine only has endermen with him. As long as we don't enrage them, they won't bother us." Crafter turned to some of the warriors nearby. "Send out the word: Do not attack the endermen, no matter what. You got it?"

They nodded their square heads.

"Then go!"

The warriors sprinted off in all directions, spreading the instructions throughout the village.

"How long do you think we have?" Gameknight asked.

"They'll wait until dark," Digger said. "So that means that we have—"

"ENDERMEN!" one of the archers shouted from the tall stone towers.

Looking out on the grassy plain, Gameknight could see a dark red creature materialize in a fog of purple haze that seemed to reach up and kiss the sky. Raising a long dark arm, the monster pointed straight at Gameknight999, then let loose a spine tingling cackle that made everyone cringe.

Gameknight reached up and closed the wooden doors, blocking out the monster, but his evil laughs passed through the walls as if they were made of air.

"It has begun," the User-that-is-not-a-user said as he drew his sword and waited for the monster of all monsters: Herobrine.

CHAPTER 12

VILLAGE IN PERIL

"I see my old friend is here," screeched Feyd from the top of the hill outside the village. "Why don't you come out and play?"

Gameknight said nothing.

"Oh, are you afraid of me?" the king of the endermen shouted. "I always knew you were a coward. Now everyone around you knows it as well."

Reaching into his inventory, Gamkenight drew his diamond sword and adjusted his diamond armor with his free hand. The enchanted sword bathed his skin with iridescent light, adding to the magical waves that pulsed across the chest plate as if both were alive. Before he could move toward the gates, a voice spoke in his ear.

"He is trying to goad you into going out there," Monkeypants said. "Don't play his game; play *your* game and be patient."

"Archers, hold your fire!" Digger yelled as he climbed the steps that led to the top of the fortified wall.

Nodding to his father, the User-that-is-not-a-user followed the stocky NPC. When he reached the top of the wall, he found Feyd still standing on the grassy plain, a faint mist of purple teleportation particles dancing about his dark red body.

"Ahh, there you are, coward," Feyd said. "I still need to discipline you for invading my home, The End. Why don't you just come down here and accept your punishment?"

"Just go away, enderman," Gameknight spat. "There is nothing here for you."

"Why, there is *everything* here for me: there is *you*." The king of the endermen cackled again, then took a step closer. "But before I can destroy you, I've been instructed to first destroy all of your friends while you watch. And when you are overwhelmed with guilt and despair at your failure to protect them, maybe then I will grant your pleas and destroy you once and for all."

"I heard the same thing from your foolish predecessor, Erebus," Gameknight shouted. "He was twice as smart as you, twice as strong, and twice as violent. He was more of an enderman than you could ever hope to be and look where all that got him. Your path of violence can only lead to your own demise, as Erebus learned in the end. Now be gone from here . . . you bore me."

"You know I won't do that," the monster said with a sneer. "My friends and I have come to erase this village from the surface of Minecraft."

"Your 'friends' . . . what friends?" Hunter yelled from one of the archer towers. She laughed and many of the other warriors joined her.

Gameknight could see the enderman's eyes begin to glow bright, his whole body starting to shake—he was becoming enraged. Quickly, the

User-that-is-not-a-user held his hands up high over his head, silencing the laughter.

With the silence, Feyd calmed down and glared up at Gameknight999.

"You want to meet my friends? So be it!" the monster shouted.

Drawing in a huge breath, the king of the endermen screeched with all his might, creating an ear-splitting sound that forced Gameknight to cup his hands over his ears and grit his teeth. Instantly, the grassy plain was filled with a purple fog that obscured the landscape. He knew that it was more endermen, but the question was: how many? With his nerves drawn tight like the string of a bow, the User-that-is-not-a-user waited for the lavender haze to clear. But before it dissipated, a familiar moaning filled the air, followed by a loud animal-like growl.

"What is that sound?" Crafter asked. "I've never heard an enderman make that sound before."

"Maybe it's a new kind of enderman," Digger suggested.

"Maybe it's . . ."

"Could it be a . . ."

Confused questions echoed all across the fortified wall as the warriors tried to understand what they were hearing, but Gameknight recognized the sound instantly. Stepping up to the edge of the cobblestone wall, Gameknight peered into the mist, dreading what he would find, but already knew what would be there.

"Xa-Tul," Gameknight growled.

"What?" Crafter asked.

The purple haze faded away, revealing a sea of endermen, each holding a zombie in their long clammy arms. Stepping away from his endermen, the king of the zombies glared up at Gameknight999, his eyes glowing like two blood-red suns.

"Xa-Tul sees the Fool is still here and has not run away like a coward," the zombie bellowed. "Perfect."

"Archers—" Digger yelled but did not get the chance to finish the command.

A roar erupted from high overhead as Herobrine dove straight for a section of the wall. Turning at the last instant, the dragon lashed out with his tail. Blocks of cobblestone crumbled away as the dragon smashed into the barricade, then turned and attacked again.

"ARCHERS, OPEN FIRE!" Gameknight yelled.

The air grew dark with pointed shafts, but the dragon was too fast. Herobrine dove at the wall with incredible speed and smashed through it headfirst. Flapping his wings with all his might, the monster climbed high into the air. As it ascended, it turned its massive head and glared down at Gameknight999, eyes glowing white with hatred.

With the wall destroyed, the zombies and endermen surged forward. But before they could reach the gap in the wall, a wave of furry white creatures darted out onto the plain and attacked—Herder's wolves.

"Wolfman!" someone shouted.

"Wolfman," said another.

"Wolfman . . .!"

The wolves tore into the ranks of zombies, their sharp teeth biting at decaying legs. Zombies flashed red as they reached out with their clawed hands at the furry attackers, but the wolves were just too fast. They streaked through the monster horde, intent on protecting this village.

Archers fired down upon the green monsters. They tried to pick off the zombies amidst the forest of tall black monsters, but eventually one of the arrows found an enderman. A painful screech sounded across the battlefield that caused all the other endermen to shout out in anger with their brother, all of their eyes now glowing bright white.

"Oh no, someone hit an enderman," Gameknight said.

"We need to fall back to the secondary defenses," Digger said, but the User-that-is-not-a-user did not reply.

Gameknight sprinted down the steps that led to the ground, both swords drawn, a look of grim determination on his square face. Moving without thinking, Gameknight999 reached the crumbled wall and stood in the breach. His swords hummed as he tore into zombies and endermen. Spinning, he attacked one monster, then before it could turn and attack, he'd roll to the side and attack another creature. Hitting one after another, he wasn't destroying them, only whittling away at their HP. The archers above took advantage of this and fired down upon the weakened monsters, consuming the rest of their health points. Creatures began to disappear around him with a *pop* as he surged forward.

Out of the corner of his eye, he saw the stocky form of Digger, his iron pickaxe carving great paths of destruction through the monster horde.

Then something hammered him in the back, sending him sprawling. Turning over, Gameknight found himself staring up into the dark face of an enderman. He swung his sword at the nightmare, but the creature disappeared in a puff of purple smoke, then reappeared at his side. Rolling across the ground, Gameknight attacked the creature's long skinny legs, slashing at them before the monster could understand where he was. The enderman flashed red as it disappeared only to reappear next to Digger. Gameknight could see the NPC was surrounded, but with three zombies charging at him, he could not help his friend right away.

Suddenly, a monkey in a superman outfit smashed into the monsters, his iron sword swinging wildly. Right behind his father came a string of warriors, all of them ready for battle. They crashed into the oncoming tide of fists and claws, ready to hold back the monsters while the other villagers moved to the secondary defenses.

"Come on!" Gameknight shouted. "We have to give the others time to get ready. FOR MINECRAFT!"

With his battle cry still resonating in his throat, Gameknight charged forward with such ferocity that it made the monsters take a step back. He smashed into an enderman, driving his shoulder into the dark creature's chest, then turned and struck a tall zombie with both swords. It disappeared with a *pop*.

"Gameknight, fall back!" someone shouted.

"Everyone, fall back to the watchtower!" the User-that-is-not-a-user echoed to his comrades fighting around him.

The warriors turned and ran, leaving Gameknight, Digger, and Monkeypants to slow the massive collection of monsters.

"Digger, Monkeypants, go!"

"Son, you can't stay here and—"

Digger didn't give him a chance to complain. Grabbing Monkeypants around the waist, he hefted him over his shoulder and ran for the tall cobblestone tower. As they fled, Gameknight backed up, placing blocks of TNT on the ground. The zombies saw the red and white striped cubes and paused for a moment. They knew exactly what they were, and none of the creatures wanted to get blown up.

"Move forward," bellowed Xa-Tul defiantly.

Gameknight could see the massive zombie king stepping through the hole in the cobblestone wall. Many of the zombies looked back at their leader in hesitation.

"Don't look at Xa-Tul, fools, ATTACK!" the zombie king roared. "Our enemy is right there." He pointed at Gameknight999 with his massive golden broadsword. "Do not let him escape!"

The zombies let out growling moans and reluctantly charged forward. Running with all his might, the User-that-is-not-a-user chanced one more glance over his shoulder. He saw a flaming arrow streak down from overhead and hit a block of TNT. The cube instantly started to blink, then erupted into flame as it tore into the zombies, throwing their bodies high into the air, leaving behind a crater filled with glowing balls of XP.

More explosions rocked the plain as Gameknight streaked for the watchtower. Endermen materialized around him, their long dark arms reaching out for him, but arrows from the rooftops drove back the creatures, leaving just enough room for escape.

When he reached the watchtower, Gameknight blocked off the door with cobblestone. Running to the nearby ladder, he climbed to the top of the tower and looked down on the village. From this vantage point, he could see the sea of monsters flowing into the village like a deadly green and black stain. They moved between the wooden structures, smashing in doors in search of any villagers hiding within their homes; there were none this time. Everyone was down in the crafting chamber, escaping through the minecart network, save for the last few defenders.

Archers on the rooftops opened fire on the monsters, both zombies and endermen. Some of the dark monsters teleported to the rooftop archer stands, but the nightmares were easily pushed off, causing them to plummet to the ground and take damage. They fired a relentless steel-tipped rain down upon the monsters, making them flash red over and over again. Flaming arrows streaked down to the ground, striking hidden blocks of explosives that blossomed into terrifying balls of flame. The archers were doing significant damage, and for a moment, Gameknight thought these last few defenders would turn back the tide . . . but then, a terrible roar echoed across the village.

Looking up, Gameknight saw the dragon swoop down again with its outstretched razor-sharp talons. Its massive tail swung and smashed into one of the archer emplacements, then the dragon struck at the warriors with its claws, knocking them to the ground below. They flashed red when they landed, and survived the fall, but a horde of twenty monsters fell on the handful of exposed defenders immediately, rending their remaining HP from them in seconds.

The dragon roared and dove toward another cluster of defenders.

"Everyone, to the crafting chamber!" Gameknight screamed, but it was too late.

Herobrine smashed into the defenders, knocking them to the ground. Gameknight lost sight when they fell, but could tell from the sounds of battle that they did not last long.

He glared up at the dragon as it circled around and headed directly for him. Not waiting, Gameknight slid down the ladder and ran for the underground tunnels. When he reached the bottom of the ladder, he found the other NPCs there, Hunter and Stitcher included. They had built tunnels from the other archer towers, making escape easier, but it hadn't worked for everyone.

"Come on, we need to get out of here!" Gameknight said.

"You think?" Hunter said sarcastically.

Stitcher punched her sister in the arm, then sprinted through the tunnel and headed for the crafting chamber. When they passed through the circular chamber and ran down the steps to the cavern floor, they found nearly all of the villagers gone; only Digger, Monkeypants, and Herder remained.

"Come on, everyone needs to escape!" Gameknight shouted.

"But my wolves!" Herder said, a look of worry on his face.

"Your wolves bought us time so that we can flee," Gameknight said. "They will escape to the woods and be alright."

Herder sighed, then nodded his head. He climbed into a minecart and disappeared into the tunnel followed by Digger and Stitcher. Hunter leaped into a minecart, then turned to Gameknight999.

"You planning on sticking around, or are you coming?" she asked.

"All those villagers . . . killed," he said in a defeated tone.

"We did what we could," Monkeypants said.

A moaning growl echoed through the tunnels overhead.

"Maybe you two could discuss this somewhere safer?" Hunter said, a mischievous smile on her square face.

"Yeah, that's probably a good idea," Gameknight replied.

"'Probably'?!" she exclaimed, then gave him a smile and shot off into the tunnel.

"Get in, Dad, you have to go first," Gameknight said.

"OK, but you're following, right?"

"I promise," he replied.

The monkey climbed into the cart and shot off into the tunnel. As Gameknight climbed into his minecart, the iron doors overhead shattered, a golden broadsword carving through the metallic barrier as if it were foil. Xa-Tul strode through the opening, his eyes burning with hatred.

"Where is the Fool going? There is still much to discuss."

The zombie king laughed, then pointed his sword down at him.

"The User-that-is-not-a-user can run away only so many times before Xa-Tul catches him."

"I defeated you once, zombie, and I will do it again," Gameknight said, but his voice lacked confidence.

Xa-Tul laughed.

"The User-that-is-not-a-user will pay for his crimes!" the zombie king growled.

Suddenly, Feyd materialized on the chamber floor. He turned and glared at his enemy and walked toward him. Gameknight quickly pushed his minecart onto the rails, then placed a block of TNT next to the tracks. Planting a redstone torch next to the red and white cube, he shot down the tunnel just before the block exploded. As the sound of the blast reverberated in his ears, he could hear Feyd screeching out in frustration.

"I will get you yet, User-that-is-not-a-user. And when I do, you will be mine!"

CHAPTER 13

FINDING HIS SONG

As Gameknight rode through the dark tunnel, he thought about the two monster kings he'd just escaped. The last time he'd fought Xa-Tul, he'd almost lost; he wasn't sure if he could defeat him again. When he'd fought Erebus, he'd been in the Land of Dreams on the steps of the Source, and he'd had Hunter and Stitcher there to help him.

But how can I fight both Feyd and Xa-Tul at once? Gameknight wondered.

And what about the dragon? He'd defeated two dragons now—one of them with an entire army at his back and the other with just his friends. But now, the dragon had all of Herobrine's powers and experience. *Can I do it again? Am I strong enough?* Feelings of uncertainty and fear wrapped around him like a leaden shroud.

Looking ahead, he could just barely see his father, Monkeypants271, his superman cape flapping behind him in the breeze. Gameknight wished he had his father's confidence.

The end of the tunnel brightened as he approached the next crafting chamber. When his cart shot into the torch-lit cavern, Gameknight saw his father placing a new minecart on the next track and shooting off into the darkness of the next passage. Crafter had already emptied this village of its inhabitants, sending them to his own village for safety. It was a ghost village now.

Gameknight picked up his minecart and carried it to the next track that would lead him toward Crafter's village. After placing it down, he climbed in and streaked through the tunnel. He would do this two more times before he made it "home."

When he finally did reach Crafter's village, he was greeted by cheering villagers. Looking around him, he was confused.

Why were they celebrating? What are they so happy about? Gameknight thought. *We were defeated.*

As he stood from his minecart, Crafter came to his side.

"What's going on?" Gameknight asked. "Why is everyone so happy? We lost that battle!"

"No, we delayed them long enough to clear out four other villages," Crafter replied. "Around you are all the NPCs we saved. If we hadn't warned them, they would still be in the path of destruction. They all know that you stayed to fight. You delayed the enemy long enough for everyone to escape."

"Not everyone," Gameknight growled.

Gameknight silenced the cheering NPCs with a glare. Slowly, he raised his hand, fingers spread wide: a salute for the dead. As he gazed around the crafting chamber, additional hands sprouted up, filling the room with extended arms and solemn faces. With his whole body filled with anger and guilt, the User-that-is-not-a-user clenched his hand in a fist. The image of those poor archers that had been attacked by Herobrine filled his mind with rage. Squeezing his fist even tighter, he could hear his knuckles pop as the sounds of their screams echoed within his mind.

Those NPCs didn't follow Gameknight to the village expecting to perish. They deserved a better fate than they received, and their deaths weighed heavily on him. He was responsible for all these people, and they were relying on him to save them. But how could he do it? He was just a kid.

Gameknight was so afraid he was going to fail that he couldn't even imagine how to try anymore. Every decision he made terrified him all the way down to his toes. All he could do now was stand in the path of the destruction and swing his swords. That's all he was good for anymore: cannon fodder.

"Well, so be it," he murmured to no one.

What he really needed was a strategic master . . . Shawny.

Monet, are you still there watching? Gameknight thought to the chat.

Yep, she replied.

I need Shawny. You think you can find him?

Two steps ahead of you, she answered. *When I saw that evil looking dragon, I called him. He's here with me and he's working on something. Hold on, he's says he's got something special just for you. You're gonna love it.*

Well, tell him to hurry. NPCs are dying down here, Gameknight answered.

He's working as fast as he can, Monet113 replied.

At least that was something.

"Gameknight, we have much to discuss," Crafter said as he approached. "We must plan what to do next."

"User-that-is-not-a-user, how should we disperse the new villagers?" Digger asked. "There's room in some of the houses, but not much. We could dig tunnels into the crafting chamber and—"

"Gameknight, we need to look at our defenses," Hunter added. "With the zombies now in the battle we can't—"

Putting his hands to his head, Gameknight screamed, silencing everyone in the chamber. He could feel a hundred pairs of eyes all looking down on him, each set expecting some kind of miraculous plan to stop the monsters and save all of their lives.

The pressure was just too much.

With everyone watching him, the User-that-is-not-a-user pushed his way through the crowd and stormed up the stairs that led out of the chamber, his entire being overwhelmed. Once he'd reached the round room where he had first met Crafter so long ago, he sprinted to the opposite side and entered the passage that would take him to the secret ladder and the watchtower. But instead of going toward the village, he went the opposite way, following a newly constructed tunnel that would take him to his own castle. Running up the stone steps, he made it into the keep of Castle Gameknight in seconds.

Stepping out into the courtyard of his castle, the User-that-is-not-a-user stared at the obsidian walls that surrounded his fortress. NPCs were placing the dark blocks on the incomplete section of the wall; that was the part he was supposed to have completed with his father, but he'd failed to do so.

Gameknight sighed.

"You know, sometimes people expect more of us than we think we can give," his father said as he approached. His ridiculous monkey face looked worried and comical at the same time. "We never really know the limits of our abilities until we try."

"But Dad, they expect me to come up with some kind of great idea that is going to save them all," Gameknight complained. "Feyd and Xa-Tul terrify me, and Herobrine is in a dragon form—that's the worst. What if I can't solve this puzzle and save them?" He lowered his voice to just a whisper. "I'm so scared that I'm gonna fail my friends that I can't even think. I'm so afraid of failing that I'm afraid to try. What am I gonna do?"

"Son, when you think about those things that scare you, they form a fog of fear around your mind, making it impossible to think. You can't focus on your fears, for fear will consume your courage and strength to fight. When you focus on what you *can* do instead of what you are afraid of, your fear will evaporate and allow you to think.

"You know, on the day your mother and I brought you home from the hospital after you were born, I felt the same way."

"What?"

"I wasn't afraid that a bunch of zombies were going to attack the house or anything like that," Monkeypants said with a little laugh. "What I mean was that it suddenly hit me that I was responsible for this new little person, and I had to teach you everything you needed to know so that you'd have a safe and happy life. I didn't know how to be a parent; I was just a clumsy engineer who liked making gadgets. I was so afraid that I would do something wrong and mess everything up. I was terrified."

"So what did you do to get over it?" Gameknight asked.

"Your mother gave me some advice that I think about every day," Monkeypants explained. "She told me, 'Every bird has a nest to tend and baby birds to care for. All the things that mama bird does for her babies are part of her song.' You see, the bird does the best it can, be it collecting food, building a nest, or singing to keep away predators. This is all part of her song. It's the same with people, but our songs are the things that we can do better than anyone else to take care of our families. Your mother's song was teaching fourth graders and taking care of us. When we brought you home from the hospital, I was uncertain and afraid, and you mother saw this in me. So she told me about the bird's song and asked me, 'What's your song?'

"I stood there in the kitchen and thought about it, then she said, 'Just be *you*, the best *you* possible. Use your strengths to do things that will help your son, for that is *your* song, and focus on what you *can* do, not what you can't.' So I started using my strengths, my song."

"What was your song?" Gameknight asked.

"Inventing, that's my song. I started putting little gadgets around the whole house . . . sensors on doors so that they'd lock if you tried to get out, special latches on the knife drawer, the robotic ball that you would chase into the bathtub. . . . I used my inventions to help you because that was my song, and I could sing that song better than anyone else in the world. You see, that's one of the goals in life, to find that thing you can do better than anyone else, your strength, your song, and then use that skill to make people's lives better.

"I stopped being afraid when I focused on what I knew I could do, which was to make inventions."

Monkeypants leaned in close and whispered into his son's ear. "What's your song?"

Gameknight looked up into his father's eyes,

"That's what you need to figure out, son," Monkeypants said, then was quiet.

Closing his eyes for a moment, the User-that-is-not-a-user thought about his father's words.

My song . . . what is my song?

Looking out the window of the keep, he could see the tall obsidian walls nearing completion. Some of the workers moved from the walls to the archer towers, placing blocks higher and higher into the air. Closing his eyes again, Gameknight imagined the army of monsters approaching the castle. There would be hundreds of endermen, zombies, and probably other creatures of the dark. The dragon would smash apart these walls in seconds. He knew, somehow, that controlling the dragon was key . . . but how? He could feel the puzzle pieces tumbling around in his head, but none of them materialized to his mind's eye; they were just a blur of possibilities.

Gameknight could see the archer towers of Crafter's village. He knew the dragon would attack there first, but it didn't seem to him that that's where the real battle would take place. Somehow, he knew that the defense of Minecraft would be fought here, in his castle. Maybe Shawny would have some ideas on how to fortify this place.

If only the users could come and help, Gameknight thought. But the ban from the Council of Crafters was still in effect; NPCs could not be seen talking or using their hands in front of users. The users had to stay out of it . . . for now.

With or without the users, the NPCs of Minecraft had to stand up and fight. What they needed was time to prepare, but who knew how much time they had?

And then an idea surfaced in the back of his mind, pushing through the fog of uncertainty and fear of failure.

"Yes, we can slow them," Gameknight mumbled, lost in thought. "We leave one person as the trigger, then he'll have to go slower, and . . ."

"Son, what are you talking about?" his father asked.

"We must slow Herobrine's army to a crawl," Gameknight said, his voice resonating with new courage.

"You found your song?" Monkeypants asked.

"I'm not sure, but I do know what we need to do next, and that's all that matters right now." Gameknight stood a little taller as he turned and headed back to the underground tunnel that would take him to the crafting chamber. "Come on, Dad, we need to get to Crafter and Digger."

Monkeypants watched his son run toward the stairs that descended deep underground and smiled.

CHAPTER 14
HEROBRINE'S PLAN

Herobrine looked over his scaly shoulder at the burning wreckage of the village as he flapped his mighty wings. Below him, the army of endermen and zombies headed east as the sun set behind them. The sky darkened to a shadowy blue, and soon sparkling stars emerged. With the sun down, the zombies were able to remove the leather caps that had been protecting them from the burning light. Without these caps, the zombies would have burst into flame in broad daylight.

"Maker!" shouted the king of the endermen up to his master.

Herobrine looked down and saw Feyd standing off, away from the other monsters. The dragon curved and banked as he approached his creation. After settling to the ground, the Ender Dragon tucked in his wings and walked next to the monster. The ever-present mist of purple and pale yellow particles of light danced about his leathery skin.

"What do you want?" Herobrine asked, a slight edge of violence in his voice. "I was deep in thought."

"I am sorry, Maker, but there are questions," Feyd said, his voice cracking with tension. "Many questions."

"Ask them then, enderman," the dragon snapped.

"We cannot continue to stay here in the Over-world," Feyd said warily. "The endermen must return to The End to regain their HP, which is get-ting dangerously low. When we teleport here, in the Overworld, we do not recover our HP. Only by tele-porting in The End do we rejuvenate."

"I know that," Herobrine replied, his voice sounding uninterested.

"And the zombies, they must return to their HP fountains in zombie-town so that they can regain their health as well," Feyd explained.

"You are not telling me anything new," Herobrine growled. "I know all of this. What is your question?"

His dragon eyes flared bright with annoyance, and Feyd stepped back, out of reach from the drag-on's razor-sharp talons.

Herobrine saw the enderman move away and laughed, then wagged his long tail, smashing it on the ground behind his shadowy servant to show him how useless his attempts to stay out of harm's way were.

The king of the endermen jumped, then bowed his head to his master.

"We do not doubt you, Maker. We just do not understand your plan." Feyd's voice sounded ner-vous. Glancing about, he could see some of his endermen warriors were watching the exchange. "Many have asked if the Maker could share his grand design for the fools of the Overworld and the eventual destiny of the monsters of darkness."

Feyd grew silent as Herobrine glared down at him, his eyes glowing with agitation.

"We mean, ahh, no disrespect," Feyd stammered, "but it is only that—"

"I will explain it to you, enderman," Herobrine said with a sneer. "I plan to destroy all of the NPCs of this world. And when I am done here, I will teleport to the next server plane and destroy the NPCs there as well, then the next server plane and the next and the next until I have purged Minecraft of this infestation."

"But to what end?" Feyd asked. "Endermen will still be relegated to their imprisonment in The End, and the zombies will still be chained to their HP fountains in their zombie-towns. How does this help the monsters of Minecraft?"

Making a vicious, guttural sound, Herobrine growled as his eyes flared with the intensity of two blazing suns. He smashed his tail down onto the ground again just behind the foolish enderman king, making Feyd flinch. The ground shook so hard that many of the endermen teleported away in fright.

Herobrine laughed. These endermen were such cowards, except for their king. That was why Feyd was so useful to him—and so dangerous. He could overcome his fear and do things that he knew to be hazardous, like go to zombie-town and confront the foolish zombie king. Herobrine knew he had to watch this creature carefully. He could be as dangerous to Herobrine as that annoying Gameknight999.

"I have not told you everything yet, enderman, nor have I shown you all of my abilities in this dragon body," Herobrine explained.

"You can do more than fly and teleport?" Feyd asked.

Some of the endermen were now returning and moving closer so that they could overhear the discussion.

"Of course, you idiot. I am an artificially intelligent virus. When my lines of code mixed with that of the Ender Dragon, it created something new and unexpected. Even the great creator, Notch, will not have expected what I have become."

The endermen moved closer, the zombies standing close behind.

"Tell us, Maker, what have you become?" Feyd asked.

"You will see soon enough," Herobrine explained, his voice booming with confidence. "My lines of code are still integrating with the software that governs the dragon. As we speak, I can feel myself changing. New abilities are beginning to emerge within me, and these will change the balance of power in Minecraft and allow the monsters of the Overworld to take over everything. But if you cowardly endermen and the sniveling zombies lack the fortitude to see this through, then run back to your prisons and stay there."

His words brought the emotions of the monsters to a simmer. Herobrine glared at the creatures and could tell that they wanted to believe him, but were still afraid. He needed to change their fear to something useful—to anger.

"I understand you are all afraid, being away from your pathetic homes, which were forced upon you by that ancient NPC, Smithy of the Two Swords," Herobrine said with a sneer. "You have been bred to live in these prisons and do as you were told by the villagers after the failed Great Zombie Invasion that happened so long ago."

Some of the zombies growled in anger. Their punishment after that failed invasion was a sore spot for all monsters. The NPCs had severely punished the monsters of the night by banishing them from the clear blue sky and forcing them to stay forever shackled to their prisons. Looking about, Herobrine could see the anger simmering within the creatures, making them grow more violent.

Good, he thought.

"You cannot be held responsible for being afraid. The monsters of the Overworld were imprisoned to the darkness long ago, long before you were created." Herobrine extended his long neck, raising his massive head high off the ground so he could stare down upon his warriors. "It is understandable that a frightened animal will become accustomed to his cage, maybe even miss it. This does not make you a coward."

Angry moans filled the air as the zombies grew more enraged, not at Herobrine, but at the victors of that ancient conflict; their captors and wardens. Looking across the faces of his troops, Herobrine could see many of the endermen were beginning to show jagged teeth, their mouths open and their eyes glowing bright with fury.

"So you have two choices: stay in your cages," Herobrine continued, "or follow me and break the chains of your oppressors. However, if you run back to the safety of your prisons, you must stay there, for I will not have cowards in my army. Run away now and never return, or stay at my side and fight the injustice that was levied upon you long ago. What is your decision?"

Zombies growled louder, the simmering emotions now boiling over. The zombies, moving as one, stepped forward and bowed to their Maker. The endermen then bowed deep as their eyes blazed with anger. Herobrine stared at Feyd, his general. The king of the endermen still appeared to be undecided. He was about to comment on Feyd's obvious contemplation when a strange sensation started to well up within the dragon. He felt as though a fire were growing within his stomach, a burning sensation that somehow felt controllable and . . . good. Drawing the bile into his mouth, the dragon spat the vile poison to the ground. Where it struck, the grassy block slowly faded from a healthy green to something pale and mottled. The color faded to an insipid yellow, and the block displayed a pattern that looked similar to cobblestone.

Feyd looked down at the block, then back up at the dragon. Herobrine could see recognition come across the monster's dark face. Instantly, the enderman teleported to the faded block, though it was only three steps away. When he materialized, Feyd looked up at Herobrine and smiled, looking rejuvenated.

"I understand your plan now, Maker." Feyd said as he smiled an evil grin. "The monsters of the Overworld are your obedient servants. We will follow you anywhere."

"Excellent," growled Herobrine. "Let us find our next victims and punish them."

With a nod of his head, Feyd silently commanded his endermen to find the next village. And as the dark creatures teleported away on the wings of tiny purple particles, Herobrine laughed an evil malicious laugh.

"I have a little surprise for you, User-that-is-not-a-user," the dragon roared.

Feyd looked up at the Maker and cackled, his eyes glowing bright.

Leaping up into the air, Herobrine beat his large leathery wings and climbed high, soaring above his army of monsters. Looking across the landscape, he instantly identified that they were in a pine forest, and an extreme hills biome sat on the other side of the next hill. Climbing higher, he looked at the patchwork of different lands that surrounded them and smiled. Curving downward again, he soared just over the treetops.

"Soon, all of these biomes will be the same," Herobrine roared. "I will bring order and uniformity to this land. And when the villagers are all extinct, the endermen will be able to live in the Overworld forever, without ever needing to go back to The End. Minecraft will be ours and Gameknight999 will be destroyed."

The dragon released a booming laugh that sounded like explosive thunder. It shook the ground and made the very landscape quake in fear.

CHAPTER 15

PREPARING THE RUSE

Gameknight entered the crafting chamber and was shocked at what he saw. NPCs were streaming in through the Minecart network; refugees from villages that had been attacked and destroyed by Herobrine and his band of monsters. They were flowing into the chamber, unstoppable. Haggard and scared from their ordeals, the NPCs' square faces broadcasted looks of terror and disbelief.

All crafting had stopped, creating an eerie silence in the chamber where the only sound heard was the clatter of the minecart wheels on the iron tracks. Crafter's workers were working as hard as they could, helping people out of minecarts and trying to ease their fears and sorrow, but the flood of emotions was overwhelming.

"My son—has anyone seen my son?" one mother asked, her face a visage of grief. "They killed my husband—my love—but where is my son?"

The woman wept, her sobs filling the silence with an overwhelming sadness. Her tears were the first of the dominoes to fall; other villagers began crying out for their loved ones, the sounds of sorrow and dread filling the air.

Then one of the refugees saw Gameknight999 at the top of the cobblestone stairs that led to the chamber floor.

"The User-that-is-not-a-user is here!" someone shouted.

Suddenly, their fears seem to subside.

"He'll stop them . . ."

"The monsters are in for it now . . ."

"Punish them . . ."

The villagers all shouted up at him; their hopes of safety and revenge piling up on him like a massive load of bricks.

Gameknight held up his hands to calm the villagers, silencing them. Scanning the crowd, he found his young friend, whose bright blue eyes and blond hair stood out in the throng.

"Crafter, get these people to my castle!" Gameknight shouted. "There is room for everyone there. The chests in the keep have food and supplies." He turned to a group of NPCs. "Builders, create rooms for all these families and be certain everyone has a home. Make sure all are cared for."

Crafter turned and looked at a group of NPCs. Nodding his blond head, he signaled for them to follow Gameknight's commands. Having a task—moving to Gameknight's castle—gave the villagers something to think about other than their loss. This brought a sense of relief to the refugees. It reminded him of something his mother had told him long ago: "Focusing on your troubles only feeds them, giving them deeper roots into your soul. The only way to uproot them is to focus on something that can be accomplished. Even the smallest victory can drive back the shadows of dread." That's what they needed, a small victory.

Looking down at the approaching NPCs, he raised his voice so that it would pierce the clattering noise of minecarts in the chamber.

"We need Castle Gameknight prepared for battle," the User-that-is-not-a-user said. This brought the flow of bodies to a halt. "Villagers, I know your homes were destroyed, and I'm truly sorry. But your home is with us now. We will not let the monsters continue their reign of terror; they will be stopped. Right now, I need your help. The castle and the village must be prepared for battle. We need stone and sand and gravel for our defense. The walls need to be thicker and the archer towers higher. All must be prepared before the monsters reach our doorsteps. Can I count on your help?"

The scared NPCs looked at each other for a moment, some exchanging sadness for fear and confusion, then one of them, a young boy about Stitcher's age, yelled aloud: "I will help!"

Scared faces turned to the boy and were shocked at the look of ferocity on his square face.

"I'll do whatever is needed," shouted another.

"Me too."

"And me."

The young boy had ignited an explosion of shouts and cheers. The mass of terrified villagers instantly turned from a crowd of defeated individuals to an army of warriors ready to take revenge on their foe. Gameknight smiled as the villagers ran up the steps, led by Crafter's builders, all of them eager to get to the castle and begin construction.

Monkeypants patted his son on the back.

"You did that well," he said.

Gameknight999 shrugged, but still felt uncertain.

Am I really helping these people, or just delaying their destruction? he wondered.

He continued down the steps to find Crafter. Pushing through the villagers and workers, he found his friend near the side of the chamber, inspecting a new tunnel being carved into the cavern wall.

"Crafter, where have all these people come from?" Gameknight asked.

"They are the survivors of Herobrine's latest attack," the young NPC explained. "The monsters are attacking one village after another, and none of the village defenses are slowing them down."

"That's because all the villagers are trying to stand against this flood by themselves," Gameknight replied.

"We need a focused, orchestrated defense," Monkeypants agreed.

"Yeah, my dad's right. We need the villagers to stand together so that we can stop Herobrine."

"What do you suggest?" Digger boomed from behind.

Gameknight turned and found the big NPC standing behind him, an iron pickaxe in his hands.

"Their destructive path will eventually lead them here. We must be prepared. If we cannot stop the monster horde at one of the other villages, then we will make our last stand here," the User-that-is-not-a-user said.

Gameknight shuddered as he thought about an army of monsters descending upon their village. He knew that Herobrine would bring everything he had to destroy this village particularly. They would be completely outnumbered, and with the vicious powers of the Ender Dragon, their defenses would not last long. He shuddered again as tendrils of fear snaked their way through his soul.

"They will crash upon our defenses and break themselves on our walls and traps. But we need time to prepare," Crafter said. "The monster army must be slowed."

"We can go forth and delay the monsters," Digger said. "But we need more NPCs."

"I will send out Riders," Crafter said. "They will gather the people we need."

"We will need everyone we can find," Digger said. "Have your Riders say that the User-that-is-not-the-user calls everyone to the defense of Minecraft. All will be needed to stop Herobrine and his monster horde. Who knows how many monsters he will have with him when he reaches our doorstep. Let all the NPCs know that it is our ancient enemy, Herobrine, who stalks us, and he will not stop until Minecraft itself is destroyed."

By now, other NPCs had moved close enough to hear their conversation in the crowded crafting chamber. Many looked worried, but when they saw the angry, confident look Gameknight wore, they all stood a little taller.

"Riders, gather all villagers who will stand with us against Herobrine's tide of destruction," Crafter said in a loud, clear voice. "It is time that we stop letting him terrorize our friends and put him in a box somewhere!"

Put him in a box . . . Gameknight thought.

The words caused the puzzle pieces to tumble about in his head. *Yes, that was part of the solution, but how do we get him to . . .* the rest of the solution was still shrouded in mystery.

"Gameknight, you OK?"

"Ahh, what?" He turned and found Stitcher standing before him, Hunter at her side.

"You had a kinda blank look on your face," Hunter said.

"I was just thinking," Gameknight said. He turned and faced Crafter and Digger. "We need to delay Herobrine so we can get our defenses ready."

Just then, one of the NPCs walked past him with an armor stand. The thin stick-like structure could be used to hold a set of armor and, when fully equipped it looked almost like a person.

He had an idea.

"Come on, we need to get to the next village before Herobrine gets there," Gameknight said. "I have a few ideas for our friends."

"Are they incredibly dangerous and insanely crazy?" Hunter asked.

"No, not this time," Gameknight answered.

Hunter frowned and pouted. "Disappointing," she said, then Stitcher punched her in the arm

"We will have a surprise for Herobrine in the next village . . . and in the one after that, as well," the User-that-is-not-a-user announced. "We need warriors, lots of them, and armor stands, as many as we can find."

Crafter looked at Digger, clearly confused, but Gameknight ignored the questioning stares. Instead, he gathered as much armor and TNT as he could hold from the crafting benches around the chamber, a mischievous smile growing on his square face.

CHAPTER 16

RATS TO THE TRAP

Herobrine flew high in the air, his eyes glowing bright with anticipation. Another village was just over the next grassy hill, but a smattering of spruce trees blocked his view of the doomed community. It did not matter. It would all be smoky ruins soon enough.

The army of endermen and zombies approached their target quietly, staying hidden. This time, they had teleported into the shadows of the forest and were slowly weaving their way between the thick trunks. Herobrine wanted the villagers to see them march out of the woods and slowly cross the grass-covered plain, magnifying the doomed NPCs' fear and despair.

The thought of the terror these idiotic villagers would feel was just delicious.

As his troops reached the edge of the forest and started out into the open plain, Herobrine gave an earsplitting roar that carried across the landscape like angry thunder. Looking toward the village, the Ender Dragon could see defenders standing atop the battlements, waiting for their attackers to crash down upon them.

But, strangely, none of the NPCs seemed to be running about, screaming in terror. They were just standing there, like they had been waiting for the monster army to arrive.

"How very disappointing," Herobrine growled.

"What are your commands, Maker?" the king of the endermen asked.

"Attack, you fool!" Herobrine boomed. "Destroy them all. Let none survive!"

Feyd smiled, then motioned for the army to advance. A hundred monsters marched past the dragon and approached the village, the mixture of endermen and zombies creating a patchwork quilt of black and green doom that flowed over the grassy plain. Both Feyd and Xa-Tul rode their massive horses, the kings towering over their troops.

The zombies growled and moaned in anticipation of the impending battle. As they drew near, Herobrine expected arrows to rain down upon his monsters, but the wall still stayed silent.

"Be careful," Herobrine bellowed. "This could be a trap set by the User-that-is-not-a-user."

Feyd screeched some response, but Herobrine could not hear the enderman. Below him, his monsters reached the base of the fortified wall. Armored NPC defenders stood on the wall as well as throughout the various wooden dwellings that had been assembled, yet none of them were moving.

"What kind of plan *is* this, Gameknight999?" Herobrine growled. "Are you trying to bore us to death?"

Turning in a great arc, the dragon soared along the wall. The zombies smashed their clawed fists against the wooden doors that barred them from entrance. In seconds, it smashed into splinters under the monstrous attack. In the midst of the raining wooden debris, the zombies flowed into the village, while Feyd and his endermen remained outside. Xa-Tul turned and looked at the endermen, then came back out of the gates, letting his zombies move through the village first. Herobrine was sure the zombie king was letting his own troops trigger whatever trap might be within the village.

Suddenly, Herobrine saw movement out of the corner of his eye. He glared at the tall cobblestone watchtower. A stocky villager hid up there, moving cautiously to the ladder that descended to the ground. Next to the ladder was a lever tied to a line of redstone powder. The redstone disappeared into the towering structure, likely leading to some contraption built by the User-that-is-not-a-user. The villager looked up at the dragon and smiled, then reached out and flipped the lever.

"IT'S A TRAP! EVERYONE GET OUT!" Herobrine screamed, but it was too late.

Cubes of cobblestone suddenly rose up in front of the destroyed doors, the blocks riding on hidden pistons. The zombies were trapped within the village.

Bellowing in rage, Herobrine swooped down on the defenders that still stood motionless on the fortified wall. Sparks of purple and pale yellow danced about his dark skin as he plunged toward the rigid NPCs. Reaching out with his pointed claws, he grabbed one of the defenders and threw him off the wall. An armor stand smashed to the ground, the leather armor in which it was clad scattered in all directions. He looked closely at the defenders; they were all armor stands.

The village was deserted!

Suddenly, an explosion blossomed from inside the village, tearing a great hole in the ground and driving the zombies toward the blocked-off exit. And then another went off. Blossoms of fire rose up into the air as zombie bodies were thrown about like discarded dolls, flashing red when they landed.

Herobrine roared in frustration. The zombies were all crowding around the exit, pounding ineffectively on the stone blocks that prevented their escape.

More explosions sounded through the village, the blasts carving great gashes into the flesh of Minecraft. The ground around the zombies erupted into deafening fire as a massive amount of TNT all exploded at the same time. The zombies were thrown in all directions at once, HP being ripped from their bodies, leaving only small piles of zombie flesh and glowing balls of XP.

Anger boiled within Herobrine as he looked down on his defeated monsters. The yellow particles that danced about on his skin grew bright as his eyes blazed with fury. He'd probably lost fifty zombies to the User-that-is-not-a-user's trickery.

GROARRR!

Herobrine's roar echoed across the landscape.

He flew back to the grassy plain facing the village and waited for the surviving monsters to return to his side. The endermen, seeing their master land on the ground, instantly teleported to his side. There was only one surviving zombie, Xa-Tul, who rode his decaying green horse slowly away from the village to join the others. As they stood there, explosions rumbled deep underground, making the ground shake slightly before going completely silent.

"That was the minecart tunnels," Xa-Tul said. "The cowards have fled."

"Cowards?!" Herobrine growled. "I see you standing here alone, while your zombies were brave enough to go into the village. Who is the coward now?"

"Xa-Tul's job is to lead, not to die," the king of the zombies said. "When the User-that-is-not-a-user faces Xa-Tul in battle, then the king of the zombies will show why he is king. Until that time, the zombies will fight for their king, and the Maker."

"You are so courageous," Feyd said with a sneer.

"Stop your bickering," Herobrine snapped. He turned to face the dark red enderman. "I want you to bring all endermen here from The End. It is time we stopped playing with these villagers and taught them what annihilation really looks like." Herobrine turned to face Xa-Tul. "When the endermen return, they will go to your zombie-town and collect *all* of your zombies. Every monster that can walk will fight. You will scour every zombie-town and bring me all of your brothers and sisters."

Xa-Tul nodded his large decaying head.

"The NPCs have had it far too easy," Herobrine continued. "My army will be the biggest ever seen in Minecraft, and then we will spread across this land like a virus." He smiled to himself and looked at his monster kings. Clearly they did not get the clever joke. *These monsters are idiots*, he thought. Sighing, he continued. "We will crash down upon the next village like it was made of grass and sticks. No NPC will survive."

The endermen around him cackled with glee.

Herobrine flapped his wings and jumped up into the sky. As he circled overhead, he watched his endermen disappear into little purple clouds of mist. The dragon knew they would return with many of their endermen brothers. With all the zombies, his army would soon be massive.

"I will make the great zombie invasion from a hundred years ago look like a little party compared to what I plan to do to the Overworld," Herobrine said to no one.

Flapping his wings, he climbed higher and higher. Looking down upon the landscape, the Ender Dragon growled, then shouted at the very fabric of Minecraft.

"You made a mistake today, Gameknight999," Herobrine yelled. "You made me mad . . . and now you will suffer my wrath!"

CHAPTER 17

READYING FOR BATTLE

Gameknight placed the cobblestone blocks as fast as he could, but building the defensive wall still seemed like it was going at an agonizingly slow pace.

"If we had World Edit, we could do this in seconds," Gameknight said.

"What's World Edit?" Monkeypants asked.

"It's a plug-in that lets you use a wand to place a lot of blocks really fast," Gameknight explained. "If we had that, then we could build massive defensive structures and make all the villages impervious to Herobrine and his monsters."

"Defenses are never impervious to people with a strong enough desire to destroy," his father said. "The only defense to violence is communication and mutual understanding."

"There is no communicating with Herobrine, Dad. He's insane and wants to destroy everything, just because he can." Gameknight paused his construction to face his father. "I'm sure he still wants to escape Minecraft and infect the Internet, and we can never let that happen. With his advanced artificial intelligence software, he could not only destroy Minecraft but the physical world as well. He has to be stopped." He moved closer to his father and lowered his voice. "But I still haven't figured out how to stop him. Herobrine will be crazy strong, and he'll fly up high so that we won't be able to reach him, just like with the Elder Guardian."

"The Elder Guardian?" Monkeypants asked. "What are you talking about?"

"Another monster we had to fight," Gameknight explained. "It was a giant, spiny puffer fish that kept floating away from us when we attacked, making it really difficult to hit. I know Herobrine will do the same thing. How can I fight him if I can't reach him? This is impossible."

All the walls and explosives in Minecraft aren't going to be enough to stop Herobrine, he thought. *We'd need a giant net to hold the dragon down on the ground. How would we ever do that?*

Gameknight knew the NPCs were counting on him, but he needed help from someone, anyone. And then he thought about his friend in the physical world. He stepped away from the wall and his father and moved next to one of the village buildings to think.

Monet, does Shawny have anything for us yet? Gameknight asked in the chat.

He's nodding his head and smiling, Jenny replied. *I think he has something good. Ahh, wait a minute.* She went silent for a moment, then came back. *Shawny said he doesn't have anything for the dragon, but he has a bunch of surprises for the monsters.*

Well, that's something, at least. Have him teleport into the keep of Castle Gameknight. Digger and Herder will meet him there.

He's on his way, Jenny replied.

Looking across the village, he spotted Digger and Herder. Motioning to them, he ran to his two friends.

"Shawny is on his way and has some ideas for our defense," Gameknight said. "Digger, Herder, go to my castle and listen to what he has come up with. He has helped us in the past and we're gonna need him again for this battle."

"But you need us here to help with the defense of this village," Digger pointed out.

"We're just slowing Herobrine down at this village, we aren't trying to actually stop him," Gameknight said. "Our defense will be where we are the strongest, and that's at our own village. But we need something there that will stop Herobrine, and walls just won't cut it. It has to be something special, something that will surprise him. That's what we need from Shawny. Do you understand?"

"He knows how to defeat the dragon?" Digger asked.

Gameknight shook his head.

"Shawny said he has something for his monster army, though," the User-that-is-not-a-user explained. "And we'll take any help we can get."

Digger nodded his head but Herder looked angry.

"My place is here, with you!" the lanky NPC snapped.

"Herder, this is not the real battle and you know this," Gameknight said. "I have Hunter and Stitcher here to protect me, but I need you back at my castle to help Digger. If you really want to help me, then you'll do this for me."

Herder frowned, then reluctantly nodded his head.

"Thank you," Gameknight said.

But Herder did not reply. Instead, he gave a loud, shrill whistle, then knelt on the ground. Instantly, a pack of wolves emerged from between buildings and ran to him. With tails wagging and eyes looking expectantly up at him, they surrounded him with their furry bodies. Leaning down to the pack leader, Herder whispered into the wolf's ear, giving it instructions, then stood and smiled at Gameknight999.

"Go!" Herder commanded.

Like bolts of white lightning, the wolves shot out of the village and ran across the surrounding savannah, spreading out around the community in a protective, watchful ring of fur and fangs.

"My wolves will stay here and help you," Herder said. "They'll signal when they see the monsters, then nibble at their flanks as they approach."

Digger laughed and patted the skinny boy on the back, almost knocking him over. Gameknight nodded and put a gentle hand on his shoulder.

"Thank you, Herder. It makes me feel better knowing that they're out there, watching." He then turned to Digger. "I'll try to slow the monsters down, but you need to work with Shawny to stop Herobrine's army so we have a chance to face the dragon once again." Gameknight moved right up next to the big NPC. "We need Shawny's contraptions and redstone traps, or I fear our defenses will not be enough. You have to get it all built before Herobrine reaches our village, or we're lost . . . understand?"

"I won't let you down," Digger said.

"OK, go!"

Digger turned and headed for the watchtower and the tunnels that would lead him to the minecart network, Herder fast on his heels.

Looking around, Gameknight was amazed at how hard all the NPCs were working to fortify this village. They all knew what was coming and the impossible odds they would soon be facing, yet they still toiled tirelessly. It was remarkable.

"The wall is done," his father said, stepping up beside him. "I had the villagers go out into the savannah and start burying blocks of TNT. We can shoot some of the blocks and explode them when the monsters are near."

"Maybe," Gameknight replied, his voice not sounding very confident. "But that will work only on the monsters that are within bow range. We need to hit them when they are farther away too . . . somehow."

"What we need is a fuse we can light that will travel out to hidden blocks far away," Monkeypants said as he cupped his square chin in his hand, thinking.

"A fuse—that's it!" Gameknight exclaimed.

He found a group of NPCs and motioned them to approach. Talking quickly, he explained his plan, and the villagers nodded as he spoke.

When he finished, the NPCs moved to the village gates and dug through the soft dirt, starting at the walls and heading straight out into the open plains. Climbing the ladders to the top of the fortified wall, Gameknight watched the villagers. One of them dug a trench two blocks deep while another followed with redstone dust, a third covering up the redstone trace. They placed the occasional repeater to keep the redstone signal strong, then put blocks of TNT on the ground. Carefully, they covered all traces of the hidden surprises.

"What are they doing?" Monkeypants asked.

"You'll see," Gameknight replied, a mischievous tone to his voice. "A little surprise for Herobrine and his mob."

Gameknight looked at the two archer towers still under construction. But as he approached the wooden structures, a commotion sounded from the watchtower. He was shocked to see villagers streaming out of the hidden tunnel, each heavily armed and armored. A cheer errupted across the village as the other NPCs saw the reinforcements bursted from the hidden tunnels. Instantly, they went to work building more towers, several heading off to expand the walls so they could accommodate all of the new warriors.

"How about that, son," his father said as he slapped him on the back. "Where did they all come from?"

"I don't know," Gameknight replied. "Maybe they are from—"

Suddenly, one of the NPCs yelled out his name and approached. Gameknight instantly recognized the villager; it was Baker, the volunteer who had gone to the last village to trigger the TNT.

"Baker, you're alright?" Gameknight asked.

Baker nodded his head.

"How did it work?"

"I wish you could have been there," Baker said, excitement filling his normally sad eyes. "It was wonderful. The explosions took out a whole company of zombies."

"Did it get the zombie king?" Gameknight asked. The thought of facing Xa-Tul in battle still terrified him.

"No, we didn't get him, but we sure got a lot of the zombies," Baker exclaimed. "The armor stands tricked him alright. They came in really slow and weren't sure what was going to happen."

"That gives me an idea," Gameknight said.

He issued instructions to some of the NPCs, putting Baker in charge before dismissing the villagers on their new mission.

"This is really starting to shape up into a strong fortress," Monkeypants said. "Maybe we can stop Herobrine here and end this, once and for all."

"No, we're only here to slow them down," Gameknight insisted. "If I know Herobrine, he'll be really angry after the little trick we played on him at the last village he visited. He's going to come at us with everything he has. We don't have enough warriors here to put up a defense. We slow him down and run; that's the plan."

"If that is true, then how will we evacuate the village quickly when it is time to run away?" Monkeypants asked. "There is only one ladder that leads down to the crafting chamber."

"Hmm . . . you're right, Dad," Gameknight said.

And then he thought about their adventure in The End, when they'd thought Herobrine had finally been destroyed. To get off the obsidian pillars quickly, Gameknight had jumped into water, which was exactly what they needed here.

Scanning the area, he saw Farmer from Crafter's village and gave her instructions. He told her what to build and where. Nodding her gray-haired head, she ran off to collect other workers.

"How long do you think we have?" Monkeypants asked. "Maybe Herobrine isn't coming to this village."

"I'm sure he is," Gameknight replied. "He's been following a straight path, moving from where he first appeared from The End and directly toward Crafter's village. Herobrine may be strong, but he isn't exceptionally bright or clever. He will continue his march across the Overworld until he finds our village and ends up right on our own doorstep."

"He doesn't sound very nice," Monkeypants added. "I think I liked him better as a pig."

Gameknight laughed for the first time in a long while.

"Yeah, me too," he replied. "But I think if we can—"

Suddenly, a howl pierced the air. It was a proud howl, not like the sorrowful moaning of a zombie. No, this sound was from a strong furry warrior, signaling that the enemy had arrived.

"They're here!" Gameknight shouted. "Everyone to your positions. Remember the plan!"

Looking over his shoulder, the User-that-is-not-a-user surveyed the village and its defenders. They were as prepared as they could be. But would this really be enough to slow down Herobrine's army? Drawing his diamond sword, Gameknight moved to the top of the fortified wall and crouched behind one of the cobblestone blocks. His father mimicked his actions.

"Are you ready?" Monkeypants asked his son.

"Do we have a choice?"

His father shook his ridiculous looking monkey head and gave his son a smile. They *had* to slow the enemy down so that Digger and Crafter could get their village ready . . . or all would be lost.

Gripping his sword firmly, Gameknight readied himself for battle.

CHAPTER 18

THE ATTACK

As the sun slowly set on the western horizon, the sky blushed a warm orange, then a fiery red. Gradually, the twinkling faces of the stars emerged, making the sky sparkle with beauty.

If only the earth could stay as peaceful and beautiful as the heavens, Gameknight thought.

Gameknight peeked out from behind the cobblestone block. The plains remained clear of intruders, but he knew they were coming. The howls of the wolves had been concentrated directly in front of them, the furry protectors nipping and tearing at the stragglers whenever possible. He could hear moans of pain as wolf teeth found zombie flesh, the howls sounding victorious, but also closer and closer.

"They're getting close," Gameknight shouted from behind the cobblestone block. "Everyone take your position and make sure they can see you. I'll give the signal to attack."

The villagers all moved into circles of torchlight, then stood still as if they were frozen statues, weapons hidden.

Crouching low behind the cobblestone block, Gameknight glanced at his father. The letters over

Monkeypant's head were barely visible while he crouched. *Good.*

Out in the dark, open plain, the bent forms of the acacia trees could be seen in the light of the torches placed there. Their crooked shapes made the dim landscape look strange and alien, as if it were a different planet. Their shadows stretched across the gray-green landscape, some of them taking on the shapes of hideous monsters.

And then one of the shadows moved.

Gameknight instantly knew it was an enderman. The dark creature walked forward into the torchlight. Reaching down, it chuckled, then took the block under the torch, causing the burning stick to instantly go out, engulfing that section of the plain into darkness. And then all across the savannah, more shadows came to life. The dark creatures removed every block of dirt into which a torch had been placed, extinguishing them and plunging the landscape into a dark gloom. Now, only the lights on their fortified wall illuminated the soon-to-be battlefield.

"They put out all our torches," Monkeypants whispered to his son.

The User-that-is-not-a-user nodded his head.

"That's OK, we couldn't shoot out that far anyway," Gameknight explained.

Out of the corner of his eye, he saw one of the villagers move.

"Stay still!" Gameknight whispered. "Let them come to us."

The NPC froze in place and stared out at the oncoming horde.

The army of monsters moved closer. As they approached, the square face of the moon began its relentless trek across the sky, casting a silvery light across the landscape. Now they could see their enemy.

Gameknight gasped.

Before them stood hundreds of zombies and endermen, each with a look of unbridled hatred on their terrifying face.

How had Herobrine collected so many monsters? Gameknight thought.

At the back of the mob, he saw Feyd and Xa-Tul, both riding their terrifying horses. The king of the endermen was looking at the statue-like figures on the ramparts, then glanced at the obviously placed armor stands next to the village gates.

"Why aren't they attacking?" Monkeypants whispered.

"They think this is another trap like the last village," Gameknight replied. "Which is exactly what we're hoping they'll think—"

"This is like the last village," Xa-Tul boomed. "The cowards have already fled. Send in your endermen."

"Perhaps the king of the zombies should lead the attack and see if he is right or not," Feyd screeched, his voice cutting through the quiet savannah landscape like a knife.

And then a roar sounded from high overhead. Gameknight could see the monsters all look up. Glancing to the sky, all he could see was a shadowy form moving above them, occasionally blotting out the stars and moon.

Herobrine . . . he was up there, somewhere.

The dragon roared again. Reluctantly, the monsters moved forward, sensing their commander's wishes.

"Get ready," Gameknight whispered.

"Xa-Tul can see the defenders are not moving," the zombie king bellowed. "There is nothing here but armor stands and empty armor."

"The Maker wants us to destroy this village, whether there are NPCs here or not," Feyd said, his voice on edge.

"Very well," Xa-Tul sighed. "Zombies, FORWARD!"

The green decaying creatures shuffled ahead, arms outstretched. Their dark claws sparkled in the moonlight, reminding all the defenders just how deadly they could be.

"Almost there," Gameknight whispered.

Now the endermen moved forward as well, their dark bodies difficult to see, though the sparkling purple teleportation particles that surrounded them made much more manageable targets.

"Remember, don't shoot the endermen, just aim for the zombies," Gameknight said. "Pass the word."

The NPCs nodded as they heard the instruction.

"Ready . . ."

The monsters moved cautiously closer, now well within bowshot, all of the decaying creatures reluctant to repeat the last battle.

Gameknight glanced down at an NPC who stood near a series of levers. Smiling, the User-that-is-not-a-user nodded his head, then stood and faced his attackers.

"FOR MINECRAFT!" he shouted.

Suddenly, the stationary statues came to life and pulled out their bows, firing at the approaching zombies. Instantly, the ground behind the green monsters exploded.

"Switch number 2," Gameknight shouted. "NOW!"

The NPC below flipped the next lever. Underground, Gameknight knew a line of redstone had suddenly come to life, sending the signal through the shallow tunnel to the waiting block of TNT. The subterranean explosive cube started to blink, though no one could see the red and white block covered with a block of grass.

But it did not go unnoticed.

The TNT exploded under a group of zombies, throwing them into the air as their bodies flashed red.

"Do all the levers!" Gameknight shouted as he drew his bow.

More explosions rocked the ground as chaos erupted amidst the monster army.

"Hunter, Stitcher, shoot the TNT!" Gameknight shouted.

From the tall archer towers, the sisters shot at the blocks of TNT that had been buried in the ground. When their flaming arrows hit their targets, the blocks started blinking. The zombies closest tried to flee, but the crush of green bodies near them hindered their escape. The explosive blocks blossomed into large flowers of flame, wrapping their burning petals around those nearest, rending HP from the green bodies.

The NPCs cheered as the zombies scattered. The archers now stepped forward and lined the wall and multiple towers. Steel-pointed rain fell down upon the monsters, wreaking havoc. Moaning cries of pain echoed across the dry landscape as the zombies fell under the archers' relentless attack. Many tried to flee, but the oncoming wave of arrows was too great, and few survived.

A group of gold clad zombies charged forward. Gameknight could see the arrows bouncing harmlessly off their armor as they advanced.

"They'll reach the gates!" Hunter yelled. "Stop them or they'll break through."

Gameknight999 was consumed with the heat of battle, his body operating without thought. Streaking down the ladder, he ran to the wooden doors and opened one. Slipping out of the village, he closed the door behind him and stood in front of the attacking zombies. Drawing his other sword, Gameknight drew a line in the ground, then looked up at the gold-clad monsters. Thinking of his favorite movie, he yelled with all his might.

"YOU . . . SHALL NOT . . . PASS!"

This made the monsters charge forward, anxious to destroy this lone defender. But they were not facing just some NPC or user. No, they were facing the User-that-is-not-a-user.

Gripping his swords firmly in his boxy hands, Gameknight999 waited.

CHAPTER 19

THE DESTRUCTION BEGINS

The monsters charged, the light from the overhead torches making their golden armor gleam. Growling with anger, the first zombie swung his golden sword. Gameknight spun, deflecting the attack with his iron sword, then brought his diamond sword down upon the monster. The creature flashed red as it howled in pain. Another zombie attacked, but Gameknight was like a whirlwind of destruction. Spinning from one zombie to the next, he chipped away at their HP.

His father charged out of the doors and smashed into the attacking zombies. With his iron sword swinging in a wide arc, he drove the zombies back with his ferocity. Quickly the monsters realized that the attack comprised only one additional person, and they closed in. They tried to circle around the pair, but Gameknight and Monkeypants stayed close to the walls.

One of the zombies lunged at Monkeypants, but before the golden sword could reach the iron armor, Gameknight blocked the attack, allowing his father to counter. He scored three quick hits before the monster disappeared, littering the ground with armor and XP.

The duo now charged forward, pushing the monsters back. But instead, the collection of monsters split in two, half focusing on Gameknight while the others focused on the monkey. A blade whistled past his head. Turning, the User-that-is-not-a-user saw that two of the zombies had gotten behind them. They were surrounding them.

"Dad, back to back!" Gameknight shouted.

Not pausing to respond, Monkeypants pressed his back to his son's, then focused on the zombies before him. But before the monsters could run in and attack in force, the gate flung open. Hunter and Stitcher came running forward, their swords flashing like iron lightning. They smashed into the zombies, carving through their defenses and tearing HP from their decaying forms. And then more NPCs came forth, each with a sword in their stubby hands. In seconds, the zombies had become outnumbered, and in a minute, they no longer existed.

"Quickly, back inside the village," Stitcher yelled. "Archers, keep firing!"

Gameknight waited by the gates until everyone was back inside, then he moved through the doors and closed them behind him.

"Did you enjoy that?" Hunter asked.

"What?"

"You know, going out there to face a dozen zombies," she said. "Just you and your two swords."

"I guess I wasn't thinking," Gameknight explained. "I knew that I couldn't let those zombies reach the doors. . . . Sorry."

"Don't apologize; it was fantastic! The more I watch you fight, the more I think you're just like Smithy of the Two Swords from ancient times," Hunter said. "You did great! Maybe you should stop thinking more often."

"ARCHERS, KEEP FIRING!" Stitcher's voice rang out from atop one of the towers.

Gameknight ran to a ladder and climbed to the top of the wall. He found his father already there, his bow singing as he fired arrow after arrow at the intruders.

Looking out across the battlefield, Gameknight noticed that the monsters couldn't get close enough to mount any kind of significant assault. There were just too many arrows coming down upon them.

Across the plains, the User-that-is-not-a-user could see Feyd glaring at him. The king of the endermen looked furious, as did Xa-Tul. Gameknight knew that the endermen could not join the fight unless one of them was attacked, and the defenders knew to fire far away from the dark nightmares. That left only the zombies and, without support, all the decaying green monsters would eventually be defeated.

Maybe we can *do this,* Gameknight thought.

A roar sounded high overhead. Gameknight saw the glowing eyes of Herobrine as he turned in a great arc and glared down at the village. Many of the NPCs aimed their arrows high into the air, but the dragon was still too far away to hit. All they could do was wait.

And then in an instant, Herobrine swooped down toward the gates. But instead of smashing the walls with his body or tail, the dragon spat something onto the ground. It was a purple stream of liquid that seemed to sparkle with teleportation particles and something sickly yellow.

When the liquid hit the ground, it spread, flowing outward in all directions like a drop of ink placed in a glass of water. Behind the sparkling wave, Gameknight could see the ground had changed from the lush gray-green savannah grass to something lifeless and pale.

"It can't be," Gameknight mumbled.

The wave spread out farther and father, leaving more of the pale yellow blocks in its wake.

"What's happening?" Monkeypants asked.

"Herobrine spat something on the ground and now everything's changing," Hunter said.

Drawing an arrow, she fired at the now-ascending dragon, but with its massive wings beating fast, it was already out of range.

"I don't like this one bit," Stitcher yelled from her tower.

She fired an arrow at the spreading wave. It stuck in the ground right before it, but had no effect. The lavender wave and insipid yellow sparks just flowed right through the arrow, doing nothing to the feathered shaft as it passed. In seconds, the wave had reached the fortified cobblestone wall. Shimmering sparks passed through the wall, turning the cobblestone into something pallid and lifeless, though the pattern in the texture remained the same.

Gameknight knew what it was.

"The wave is turning everything into End Stone," Gameknight shouted. "Herobrine is bringing The End to the Overworld!"

The NPCs gasped.

As the wave moved into the village, those on the wall just stood and watched in horror.

"Don't just stand there, RUN!" Gameknight screamed.

But the NPCs were unable to move; they were horrified and in shock. When the transformation wave reached the nearest villager, the NPC cried out in pain as the wave flowed over him, then grew silent. When the sparkling purple field moved past the villager, all that remained was a pale yellow statue where the NPC had stood, his weapons lying on the ground at his stony feet.

"He's completely turned into End Stone," Gameknight exclaimed. "Everyone fall back, FALL BACK!"

The villagers moved off the fortified wall and away from the oncoming wave. Some were not fast enough and were trapped as the wave engulfed stairways and ladders. Without any other option, the NPCs surrendered to their fate and knelt down in defeat as the purple particles enveloped them. Wrapped in a sickly yellow glow, the NPCs transformed, leaving more cold and lifeless End Stone sculptures as the wave moved past them.

Cries of grief rose up from the NPC defenders. Many fired arrows at the approaching wave, but they did nothing. The wave just continued to advance, changing everything with its poisonous touch.

"Everyone evacuate the village!" Gameknight shouted. "To the minecarts!"

Sprinting with all his speed, the User-that-is-not-a-user darted to the watchtower. If they had to all use the secret ladder, they would be doomed, but Gameknight had planned for this eventuality. Multiple holes could be found in the floor of the watchtower, each one going straight down to a pool of water. When he reached the cobblestone structure, Gameknight saw NPCs leaping into the holes.

Far below, he could hear splashes as they landed safely in the water, then followed tunnels to the crafting chamber.

Streaking down out of the sky, Herobrine crashed through the stone wall surrounding the village, obliterating a huge portion and creating an entrance for his monsters.

The dragon glared at Gameknight999, then flapped his wings as he took to the air. Charging through the gaping hole in the fortified wall was Xa-Tul and Feyd, a sea of monsters following close behind.

More villagers were still running to the safety of the tunnels, but the transformation wave was catching too many, turning them into sad, motionless statues. Those who escaped the transformation wave found reenergized zombies and endermen waiting for them in the village courtyard.

"Come on, Gameknight, we gotta go," Hunter said as she grabbed his arm.

"Wait, I have to help the others," the User-that-is-not-a-user yelled.

But Hunter did not listen. She dragged him from the scene and shoved him into one of the many holes that had been dug for their escape. He fell down the long shaft and landed with a splash in a shallow pool of water. Standing, he moved into the tunnel as if he were in a trance. He could hear the screams of the villagers above who were unable to escape the End Stone wave. Their cries of terror hammered into his soul.

"Come on, son, we can't help anyone up there," his father said.

Snapping out of the stupor, Gameknight found Monkeypants looking at him, his comical monkey face not looking so funny at the moment.

More screams echoed down the tunnel, followed by zombie moans and the chuckles of endermen. After a few moments, Gameknight heard only monsters.

"Quickly, cover the water before the zombies get down here," Hunter ordered.

Gameknight was unable to speak or function. The lives he'd seen lost up there in the village had stunned him.

"He changed them . . . to . . . End Stone," the User-that-is-not-a-user mumbled. "How can anyone be so . . . cruel?"

Quickly, Hunter and Stitcher filled in the watery pools with stone, just as the zombies started arriving. One of the monsters managed to land in the water before Stitcher sealed it up, but it was quickly destroyed by NPCs waiting nearby. More zombies fell down the shafts, but with the water covered, the monsters just disappeared as their HP was suddenly brought to zero via their stony impact.

"They're End Stone," Gameknight mumbled, still in shock. "How could any creature do that to another living thing?"

Someone grabbed him by the arm and led him through the passages to the crafting chamber. Multiple hands tried to pick up Gameknight and place him in a minecart, but he pushed them away. The horror and shock that had overwhelmed him earlier now gave way to rage.

"How could any creature do that to another?!" Gameknight shouted. "I'm tired of this! I'm tired of Herobrine pushing us around and making us terrified all the time!"

Up near the top of the chamber, a sparkling purple line appeared. As it moved downward and forward, the walls of the crafting chamber slowly changed to End Stone as the transformation wave continued forward, unrelenting.

"How do we stop it?" someone asked, but Gameknight could not tell who it was.

He was consumed with rage.

"HOW COULD SOMEONE DO THAT!" he screamed as he drew his swords. "I WON'T ALLOW IT! I REFUSE!"

"Son, we have to go," his father whispered directly in his ear. "We can't fight this thing right now. Our only course of action is to flee."

Gameknight's vision finally cleared. He looked into his father's eyes and recognized fear. As Monkeypants glanced at the approaching transformation wave, Gameknight realized the fear was not for himself, but for his son.

"I'm done doing things that Herobrine expects," Gameknight shouted at the approaching wave.

Gameknight stood next to the minecart tracks and waited for the last few people to jump into a carts and speed down the tracks.

"Come on, son," Monkeypants said.

"I'm right behind you. Go!"

Monkeypants nodded his head, then shot down the tracks and disappeared into the dark tunnel. Gameknight climbed into a minecart and moved it next to the powered rail. Reaching out, he pushed on a lever that activated the TNT that had been spread all throughout the chamber. It would detonate in seconds.

Glaring up at the approaching purple transformation wave, Gameknight let out an animal-like growl.

"It's time to change the game, Herobrine!" he shouted. "You may know a lot about Minecraft, but I know a lot about griefing! It's time we did things my way. Prepare yourself, dragon, for the king of the griefers is about to descend upon you, and I will show no mercy."

Pushing his minecart forward, he sped down the tracks and into the darkness just before a series of explosions tore apart the minecart rails and tunnels. The enemy would not be able to follow them.

"Get ready, Herobrine. I'm coming for you!" the User-that-is-not-a-user shouted.

And in that moment, the music of Minecraft swelled.

CHAPTER 20

HP FOUNTAINS

Herobrine roared with laughter as his transformation wave moved through the village and out into the savannah plain. The dragon was just as surprised by what had happened as the villagers had been. Changing the Overworld into The End had been an unexpected development, and he was very pleased with his new power.

As the wave spread out in all directions, Herobrine noticed dark patches of purplish-black forming on the ground. As he watched, wide pillars slowly sprouted up out of the pale surface like budding plants. Obsidian pillars! Likely when they reached full height, an Ender Crystal would materialize at the top, bathed in flame.

Good, I'll need the healing powers of my Crystals, Herobrine thought.

Soaring high up into the air, the Ender Dragon looked down at his troops. His endermen were teleporting across the newly formed End Stone, each one collecting HP from the teleportation particles that surrounded their dark bodies. Normally, the purple particles would not have nourished the endermen while in the Overworld, but this was no longer the land of the NPCs. Herobrine had turned the dimensions of Minecraft upside down, bringing complete chaos to the server.

Spotting his dark red general below, the dragon gracefully arced to the ground and settled before the king of the endermen.

"Feyd, that battle did not go well," Herobrine said.

"We won, Maker. How much better could it be?" Feyd asked.

Herobrine's eyes glowed bright white with annoyance as he gave the enderman an angry glare.

"Where is that fool, Xa-Tul?" Herobrine growled.

"He's somewhere in the village," Feyd asked, bowing his head respectfully and nervously.

"Bring him quickly, and do not make me wait. My patience is short."

The enderman disappeared in a cloud of purple mist and quickly returned with the zombie king at his side, facing backward, a dark red hand on the zombie's shoulder.

"What is the meaning of this?" the zombie bellowed as he reached for his sword. "Xa-Tul was inspecting the victory brought about by the zombies. Xa-Tul demands to be treated with the respect deserving of a conquering hero."

"Be quiet, you fool," Herobrine snapped.

The zombie king turned around and was surprised to find Herobrine there. Quickly, he bowed his head, trying to show enough respect to avoid the dragon's temper.

"Now both of you listen," Herobrine said. "That battle was pathetic. Their archers kept us out of the village. If I hadn't intervened, then the NPCs would still be in control. We need something to neutralize their archers." The dragon paced back and forth as his eyes grew bright, deep in thought. His mighty paws made the ground quake as he paced, but then suddenly, he stopped and turned his massive head toward his generals. "We need our own archers. We need the skeletons."

"They still hide in their tunnels, Maker," Feyd said. "The sniveling creatures are afraid of the User-that-is-not-a-user because of the Last Battle."

"The Last Battle hasn't happened yet," Herobrine snapped, his eyes glowing brighter.

"But they do not know that," Feyd said.

Herobrine growled, then turned and faced the zombie king.

"Your troops were pathetic," the dragon said. "Since they cannot fight well, we have to make up for their shortcomings with numbers. You will bring more zombies here, to this spot."

"But Xa-Tul emptied many zombie-towns to give you the army that you had," the zombie king explained. "When the others learn of the losses at this—"

"Do not tell them of the losses!" Herobrine boomed. "Order them to come, or destroy them. You will take a company of my endermen with you. I know of the portals that connect all of your underground towns. Use the portals and bring all of them here. If any refuse, destroy them."

"But how are we to survive up here on the surface?" Xa-Tul asked. "The End does not give us sustenance as it does the endermen. We cannot survive for long away from our zombie-towns."

Herobrine growled, then closed his eyes. Concentrating deeply, he gathered his crafting powers, causing his front paws to glow. Reaching out, he plunged his clawed fingers into the pale End Stone. Slowly, an insipid sickly looking yellow glow radiated outward. Instantly, a tiny green dot formed in front of the dragon, and emerald sparks burst from it. When they landed on the zombie king, Xa-Tul smiled and moved closer.

Reaching deeper into the ground, Herobrine pushed his crafting powers harder until pure white spots formed on the End Stone as well. These tiny bleached circles instantly brought forth glistening white embers, similar to those of the zombie HP fountain, but completely white instead of emerald green.

Herobrine drew his hands from the pale soil and looked at his kings, an evil smile on his dragon face.

"Tell the skeletons there will be HP fountains up here for them as well as for the zombies," Herobrine explained. "I have promised the Overworld to the creatures of the shadows. Here is my proof."

Feyd chuckled, his own eyes glowing white with glee.

"Bring me my soldiers," Herobrine added. "I want three hundred skeletons and three hundred zombies here within a day or I will be upset. And when I get upset, I might get the irresistible urge to destroy a general. Let's see who disappoints me first."

Flapping his mighty wings, Herobrine leapt up into the air, leaving his terrified generals on the ground below. As he rose, he watched his transformation wave stretch out in all directions, a sparkling purple and yellow ring moving at walking speed across the Overworld. Behind the lavender ring, everything was a beautiful pale yellow: trees, plants, pigs, cows . . . Everything turned to End Stone.

Herobrine laughed.

Soon, his transformation wave would engulf all of Minecraft, but he had to reach the User-that-is-not-a-user first. *He* wanted to be the one to destroy that foolish user. Herobrine had much to punish him for, and he didn't want the transformation wave to steal from him the glory of Game-knight999's destruction. That would not do at all.

CHAPTER 21

FINDING COURAGE

When Gameknight stepped out of the mine-cart in Crafter's village, the warriors from the battle were all talking about The End, each tale becoming bigger and more terrible than the last. Tearful stories were relayed of friends and neighbors who couldn't escape the poisonous tide of transformation. Silent statues now marked their passing.

Gameknight could see fear and uncertainty in their eyes, and he understood why. What they had witnessed was horrifying. Their friends had been transformed from living NPCs to stone in the blink of an eye, and all because of their enemy, Herobrine.

The image of that monster popped into his head; pointed teeth, razor-sharp talons, spiked tail . . . those blazing white eyes. Everything about the creature was terrifying and he reminded Gameknight of the bullies at school, especially Skorch, the big red-headed kid in eighth grade. He was so tired of bullies pushing him and his sister around at school, in the neighborhood, at the park . . . and now in Minecraft.

He'd had enough!

When Gameknight thought about facing Herobrine, his blood turned to ice. But he knew that if he did nothing, then the outcome here was guaranteed; all of these NPCs would perish.

I must help them, Gameknight thought, *even if helping them means facing Herobrine and his monster kings.*

Turning to the throngs of terrified NPCs, Gameknight found Crafter amidst the panicking villagers and moved to his friend's side. Stepping up on top of a block of stone, Gameknight shouted to get everyone's attention. They did not hear him. Placing another block under him, he rose higher, and with another block, even higher.

"Quiet!" he yelled as he banged the side of his diamond sword against the stone cubes beneath his feet. "QUIET!"

The NPCs all stopped talking and looked up at the User-that-is-not-a-user.

"I know what we just witnessed was terrible," Gameknight said in a sad voice. "It was beyond anything any of us could ever imagine, but we cannot lose hope."

Spreading his fingers wide, he reached up high into the air, extending his arm as far as it would go, then clenched his hand into a fist. A hundred villagers followed his example. Thinking about Herobrine, Gameknight squeezed until his knuckles turned white.

"We will not let Herobrine get away with this!" Gameknight finally said, his eyes filled with fiery rage. "He *will* be brought to justice."

"But he's the Ender Dragon. He's too strong."

"We should just run away . . ."

"Yes, he is strong, but we cannot run away," Gameknight said. "Running away from a problem never solves anything. It will only make the problem worse. No! I say we face him again and again until we can finally stop him here, at our village."

"But what if—"

"There is no 'What if'!" the User-that-is-not-a-user cried. "There is only now! And right now, you all need to decide if you are with me in this or not." Putting his sword back in his inventory, Gameknight jumped down and walked amongst the villagers. "I am going to fight Herobrine until he is defeated. What we've done already hasn't worked. We've been trying to stop him with walls and swords, arrows and fortifications." He paused to scan the crowd, looking for his father. "Dad, what's rule number 2?"

"Rule number 2: If what you're doing doesn't work, try something different," Monkeypants quoted.

"Exactly," Gameknight said. "We realized now that we can't fight Herobrine with just armor and swords; we need to try something different.

"Now, as many of you know, I have a shadowy past," Gameknight said, lowering his voice. "I was a griefer. I did terrible things in Minecraft to both users and villagers alike."

Just then, Digger and Herder entered the crafting chamber and stood on the long stairway that led to the floor. Gameknight looked up at the big NPC and clasped his fist to his chest, then bowed to him, apologizing again.

"I took Digger's wife from him with my selfish griefing behavior, because I was a fool. I even griefed this village on numerous occasions, all because I was an idiot."

"You can say that again," Hunter added.

Stitcher gave her older sister an angry stare, silencing her.

"But there was one thing I was certain of back during my griefing days," Gameknight said. "Do you know what it was?" He paused, giving the villagers time to think. "I was really good at griefing . . . maybe the best . . . the king of the griefers. I'm not proud of those days, but I know that I was better than anyone else at ruining PvP games, destroying castles, stealing stuff. I was the king of the griefers and no one could compete with me."

The NPCs looked at each other, confused.

"Well, it's time we put those old skills to use. It's time we griefed Herobrine," the User-that-is-not-a-user stated. "Dad, what's rule number three?"

"When something *is* working, don't change anything," Monkeypants stated.

"That's right. I know my griefing works, because I did things to people, terrible things, and always got away with it. Now it's time to use my griefing for good, to turn it on Herobrine. I am going to grief him over and over until he is overwhelmed with frustration. Because of my griefs, he will be forced to slow his attacks to a crawl, giving us time to prepare for the final showdown.

"Now I understand that many of you are afraid. . . . I'm scared, too, but you can't just run and hide. That transformation wave will eventually find you . . . find all of us."

"Then how will you stop that wave?" someone asked from the crowd.

"I don't know," Gameknight replied. "But I am certain that if we just give up and hide, then we are doomed."

The NPCs grew silent.

"If we do nothing, then the outcome is guaranteed," Gameknight stated. "If we do *some*thing, then maybe we can change our fates. What I'm going to do is slow down Herobrine by griefing him every chance I get while those who remain here prepare the village and the castle." He walked through the crowd, looking into the rectangular eyes of each scared NPC. "I know you're afraid of that transformation wave . . . only an idiot wouldn't be. I'm afraid of it too, but I'm more afraid that I might let all of you down and not be the User-that-is-not-a-user that you all need me to be. But if I do nothing . . . well, we know what would happen then, and that's unacceptable."

He looked up at Digger, who clenched his hand in a fist and pounded it against his chest. It sounded like thunder echoing through the crafting chamber. Herder did the same, creating another burst of thunder. Many of the NPCs looked up at the two villagers, but fear still ruled their minds.

Gameknight smiled up at his friends.

Pushing through the crowd, Stitcher moved to his side and she slammed her fist against her armor, turning to glare at the other NPCs.

"I know that I can give Crafter, Digger, and Herder the time they need to get this village prepared for battle. I cannot do it alone," Gameknight said. "But if I must . . . I *will* face Herobrine on my own."

"No, you won't," Monkeypants said as he pushed through the NPCs to stand at his son's side. "There will at least be two of us next to you." His father looked down at Stitcher and smiled at her, then clenched his hand into a fist and slammed it against his iron chest plate.

"I'm not missing the fun," Hunter said, her fist pounding on her chest. "We're with you, Gameknight999. And just so we're clear, the only way you can *not* be the person we need is if you give up and stop trying."

Gameknight smiled at his friend, then turned to face the rest of the villagers. He could still see fear filling their eyes—fear of the transformation wave and fear of Herobrine.

Gameknight sighed.

"Well . . . if you won't help me, then—"

"NO!" cracked an aged voice.

Pushing through the crowd, Gameknight saw Farmer coming toward him. The old woman had been in the first village to fall to Herobrine's army. She had lost everything to the monsters, and yet she was still here fighting.

Shoving her way forward, she stepped up to Gameknight999.

"Give me your sword," she snapped, her wrinkled eyes filled with intense rage.

Gameknight drew his iron sword and offered it to her, hilt first. The old woman tried to lift it up over her head, but it was too heavy. Instead, she held it with both hands and raised it up as high as she could. The tip of the blade made it just to her shoulder height, causing the other villagers to step back.

With the blade wavering in her hands, she spoke.

"What's wrong with you people?" she shouted at the villagers. "These monsters are going to take everything from you, your village . . . your loved ones . . . even Minecraft. If you need it, I will stand with you, Gameknight999. My sword will be there at your side, even if I can't quite hold it up for very long."

Her tired arms finally gave out and the sword clattered to the floor. Gameknight bent and picked it up with his left hand, then drew his diamond blade with his right.

"It's OK, Farmer, I can hold your sword for you," the User-that-is-not-a-user said.

Farmer moved in front of Gameknight.

"Then I will use my body as your shield," she croaked in an aged, scratchy voice. "You will not be alone on the battlefield."

The villagers looked at the old woman with shock and wonder in their eyes. Many of them nodded their blocky heads as they stared at Farmer, their fear replaced with pride.

A young boy Gameknight had never seen before moved forward to stand in front of Farmer, using his small body to protect the old woman. A planter then pulled out her hoe and stood next to Farmer, a look of grim determination on her face.

"You will not be alone," Farmer said, slamming her fist to her chest. "I'll be at your side."

"You will not be alone," said another.

"I'll fight with you . . ."

"I'm with you . . ."

An avalanche of bravery crashed down upon the NPCs, all triggered by the withered form of an old farmer. With fists slamming against chests, the terrified villagers transformed themselves, by the strength of their will, from a collection of terrified individuals to an army of fighters, ready to battle for their freedom against an unstoppable foe.

The chamber filled with thunder as fists crashed against leather, iron, and diamond. They all knew their chances of success were slim, but with the User-that-is-not-a-user at the head of their army, they all had something that Herobrine could not take away from them: hope.

CHAPTER 22

DESERT BATTLE

Standing on the sandy wall, Gameknight peered out into the darkening desert, watching for the predator that he knew was stalking him: Herobrine.

With the newly-energized NPCs, Gameknight and the villagers had emptied three more villages in Herobrine's path and brought them all here to this village in the desert. He'd been preparing a massive grief against Herobrine. TNT and other traps had been distributed all around the village. They had labored for days, digging holes, running redstone powder, setting traps, and finally they were ready.

But these preparations hadn't just been for the village. NPCs were replicating their efforts in the next four villages as well, creating a line of booby traps that led all the way to Crafter's village.

To make his griefs as effective as possible, Gameknight needed the monsters so mad that they'd charge forward when they saw him. As a result, the cavalry had gone off to harass the enemy during its long trek across Minecraft. They attacked the monster army's flanks and rear while NPCs set traps ahead of them. With tripwires and pressure plates tied to TNT and arrow dispensers, the traps hadn't done a lot of damage, but that hadn't been their intent. Their purpose had been to troll them, making them mad and careless. Based on the reports he'd received from the returning warriors, it was working beautifully. The monster army was now infuriated and wanted nothing more than to destroy every NPC they saw.

Looking out across the desert, Gameknight could see the last preparations being completed. Warriors were climbing out of trees that Treebrin had planted, while Grassbrin was finishing placing lines of dirt that would hold his long green snares. A wide moat was being filled around the desert village; the water, though only four blocks deep, would be wide enough to keep the endermen from approaching.

They were ready.

Looking to the west, Gameknight could see the sun's square face start to kiss the horizon. Normally, the night would have made the villagers nervous, but this time, they wanted the darkness. Their pressure plates and trip wires would be harder to see.

Suddenly, a firework shot into the sky, exploding in a burst of green sparks that formed the face of a creeper. One of the monsters had stepped on a tripwire.

They were here.

"Everyone get to your positions!" Gameknight shouted. "Archers to the walls and towers. We'll easily keep the zombies back from the walls, but be ready for the dragon. When he spits his purple poison and turns the desert to End Stone, that will be our signal to flee."

Looking behind him, Gameknight could see pools of water all throughout the village, especially around the archer towers. Ladders took too long to climb down, they'd found, so instead the warriors would jump into pools of water to get down from their battle stations and run for the minecarts when it was time to retreat.

Another firework shot into the sky, this one bursting into a large orange sphere.

"They're almost here. Get ready!" Gameknight shouted.

"I see them!" Stitcher shouted from the tallest archer tower. "They're just moving over the largest hill and they are . . . oh my."

Gameknight looked up at his friend and could just barely make out her face in the darkening light of dusk. She was clearly shocked, staring out at the approaching mob.

"Stitcher, what is it?" Gameknight shouted. "What's wrong?"

She looked down at her friend, her face almost white with fear.

"There are a lot of them," she said. "I mean, A LOT! There must be hundreds of zombies and endermen, but also skeletons as far as the eye can see."

"Skeletons?" Gameknight asked.

She nodded her head.

"Well, we can't do anything about it now," Gameknight said, then turned and looked at the villagers. "Stick to the plan and be ready to evacuate."

Glancing about the village, Gameknight saw that the NPCs were all grimly determined, even if it looked somewhat forced. The NPCs were still scared inside, and the only thing holding that thin strand of courage together was Gameknight999.

The User-that-is-not-a-user forced a smile to his square face as he looked into their faces.

"These people have faith in you, son," his father said next to him. "They believe in you even though they all know that nothing is guaranteed. What they do know is they have a chance as long as Gameknight999 is with them."

"But what difference can one person make?"

What difference can one arrow make? Monet113 asked through the chat.

Gameknight smiled and nodded his head. In their battle with the spider queen, Shaikulud, he had said that very thing to his sister. And in the end, her one arrow had saved his life and destroyed that terrible monster.

"It isn't your sword that will make the difference, son," Monkeypants said. "It is your presence. Your tenacity and unwillingness to yield to this monstrous tide gives them hope and boosts their courage. Hope can be a powerful weapon."

"But Dad, some of them might not survive," Gameknight whispered, leaning close. "How do I keep them all safe?"

"It's not your job to take responsibility for all their fates. It is your job to give them courage and a chance. They all know the danger before them, but they believe in their cause and are willing to take this risk. Your job is to respect the sacrifice they are all willing to make, to be brave and lead these people to victory."

Be brave? What a joke. I'm terrified, he thought. *Look at all those monsters out there.*

Across the desert, the mob flowed over the far sand dune. The pale desert was slowly becoming colored black, green, and white as the endermen, zombies, and skeletons spread across the landscape like a virus, extending tendrils of hatred and spite to everything they touched. There must have been two hundred of them, if not more.

How am I supposed to stop that many?

Just then, a roar bellowed from behind the monsters . . . Herobrine. The NPCs all gasped as the dragon shot up into the air from behind the murderous horde. Beating his leathery wings, he climbed into the air and disappeared into the darkness.

"Everyone get ready!" Gameknight yelled as ripples of fear cascaded down his spine.

Every NPC drew their bows and aimed high into the air.

"NOW!" Gameknight screamed.

As one, the villagers fired into the darkness. Watching the enemy, Gameknight could see the monsters following the flight of arrows with their dark, lifeless eyes. He could tell that the horde was still out of range and that they had to get them closer to the walls.

At first the sight of the arrows made the monsters panic, but soon they realized the arrows were not going to hit them. In fact, they were not even aimed at them at all. Rather, the arrows were flying to the left and right of their positions, the pointed projectiles unable to reach their enemy.

The mobs started to laugh as the arrows flew to the side, landing harmlessly into the sand, but a few of them found their targets. Arrows landed on the many pressure plates hidden in the dunes, triggering redstone circuits. Suddenly, the grinding sound of pistons moving echoed across the desert. Individual square holes opened within the monster's formation and TNT blocks popped up into the air and exploded. Skeletons and zombies were thrown into the air as endermen teleported to safety. Some of the endermen flashed red as they took damage, but did not become enraged because they had not been directly attacked.

Rather than cheering, the villagers laughed.

"Fire again!" Gameknight shouted.

Another volley of arrows soared through the air, these even farther to the sides of the battle-field. When they landed in the ground, more red-stone circuits activated, triggering blocks of TNT at the rear of the enemy. Violent balls of fire erupted behind the enemy formation, driving them forward.

"Excellent," Gameknight whispered.

Angry moans came from the zombies as they advanced, the clattering of the skeletons adding to the terrible battle sounds. The monsters had furious looks on their faces, their cold dead eyes all focused on their enemy, the User-that-is-not-a-user.

On top of the far dune, Gameknight could see the three generals—Feyd, Xa-Tul, and the new addition, Reaper, the skeleton king—all sitting atop their horrifying monster horses, watching the battle and shouting commands.

If only there were some TNT under them right now, Gameknight thought then grew angry. *I should have thought of that!*

The monster army surged forward, the skele-tons starting to open fire on the defenders stand-ing atop the fortified wall. Villagers ducked behind blocks of sandstone and cobblestone as arrows streaked past. Cries of pain sounded from the bat-tlement as some of the enemy arrows reached their targets.

"Keep firing!" Gameknight shouted. "Drive them back."

But the monsters continued forward. As they fired their deadly bows, the skeletons drew near Treebrin's trees. Eventually, one of the monsters hit tripwires stretched across the battlefield. Attached to the tripwires were redstone circuits that drove dispensers hidden in the treetops. Streams of arrows fired from the dispensers, tearing a painful gash into the army.

"Hold your fire!" Gameknight shouted.

The archers on the walls stopped their assault as the monsters tried to move away from the lethal trees. They ran to the left, away from the dispensers and toward the next trap.

Gameknight smiled.

The creatures hit another series of tripwires and pressure plates. TNT erupted under the feet of the monsters, turning the desert into a world of fire and smoke. Great balls of flame blossomed under the monsters, making the creatures flash red as they disappeared, leaving behind glowing balls of XP. The huge explosion shook the world as if the massive fist from some mythical giant had hammered down upon the sandy ground.

Gameknight smiled again. The monster horde had probably been cut in half.

But then a screech sounded from the far dune. Glancing up, Gameknight could see Feyd, the king of the endermen, glaring at him, his white eyes filled with hatred. Motioning to something behind him, he slowly advanced, the other monster kings staying at his side. As the three mounted leaders moved forward, another massive collection of monsters flowed over the dunes.

"There's *more* of them!" someone shouted.

"Oh no!"

"What do we do, what do we do?"

Their traps had been sprung. The bouncing TNT bombs were still going off, but the monsters wisely stayed far away. The dispensers in the trees had exhausted their ammunition and all that came from the dark chests were puffs of air.

"Archers, open fire!" Gameknight shouted.

But another army of skeletons flowed over the dune and fired upon the desert village. Two hundred arrows rained down upon the defenders, tearing HP from NPCs, causing many to disappear with a *pop*. Looking around at the village, Gameknight could see items begin to litter the ground as NPCs ceased to exist under the massive wave of enemy arrows.

The defenders fired down on the monsters as they advanced, but with the constant flow of arrows falling down on them, most had to stay hidden behind blocks for protection.

"They've reached the moat!" Hunter yelled from one of the archer towers.

"Don't worry; they can't cross it," Gameknight yelled.

Suddenly, he saw a strange-looking figure emerge from the desert. He was clad in a dark midnight blue smock with a sky-blue stripe running down the center. In the darkness, it was difficult to see the creature's face, but in the moonlight, Gameknight could see his hair was a light blue, the tips of his locks a frosty white.

The creature moved to the moat and placed his hands in the water. Instantly, the moat turned to ice, allowing the zombies to easily cross to the gates. The endermen, seeing the safe crossing, teleported to the moat and started to cross, as well.

"That looks like an NPC down there," Stitcher yelled, pointing at the blue stranger. "What is he doing?"

The younger sister looked at her older sibling and pointed at the stranger.

"He turned the water to ice. How did he do that?" Stitcher asked.

"I don't know and I don't care," Hunter yelled. "I'm putting a stop to it!"

She raised her bow and aimed at her target. But just before she could release the arrow, the stranger looked up at Hunter and smiled. Flashing an icy grin, he pulled his hands out of the ice. Instantly, the frozen moat turned to liquid again, causing the zombies and endermen to fall into the watery trap. The endermen flashed red as the water tore into their HP and the zombies quickly sank to the bottom.

More of the archers turned their bows to the newcomer, but Hunter stopped their attack.

"Wait, he's a friend," Hunter said as she nodded at the strange NPC.

Just then, the main skeleton force advanced, firing a nearly constant flow of arrows that drove the defenders from the fortified wall. Overhead, the dragon roared and swooped down on the battlefield. As it neared the desert floor, Herobrine spat a long stream of purple poison that hit the sandy ground in front of the village and instantly transformed it to End Stone. The purple transformation wave immediately spread, the sparkling purple distortion turning Treebrin's trees to pale yellow stone with its horrific touch.

"Everyone, run for the minecarts!" Gameknight screamed.

Herobrine climbed high into the sky, then turned and streaked down, picking up speed as he plummeted. Turning sharply when he neared the ground, the flying monster headed straight for the village, his body enveloped with purple and pale yellow embers. He accelerated, then spread his leathery wings and glided toward his target. Archers tried to reach out with their arrows, but the dragon was moving too fast when he streaked over the fortified wall. Gameknight saw the monster's eyes glow bright when he spat his deadly poison on a cluster of villagers, the yellow glow around him growing momentarily bright. The villagers held up their weapons, hoping to somehow deflect the attack, but their defenses were useless. They were instantly turned to End Stone, a look of surprise and fear permanently frozen on their stony faces. Firing again, he hit a group of archers atop one of the village buildings, their bodies now permanently fused to the transforming building with End Stone.

Herobrine flapped his wings and climbed as he flew out of the village, but turned quickly for another pass. Slicing through the air, the dark beast dropped his deadly poison again, catching NPCs as they ran for the safety of the watchtower. He was like an aerial dive-bomber, strafing the NPCs without remorse. Villager after villager screamed out in terror and were then cruelly silenced.

Gameknight watched the carnage unfold, his mind consumed with terror. Herobrine was destroying the NPCs, and every spit of his poison caused the transformation wave to spread faster through the village. Avenues of escape were being cut off, leaving many trapped with no other option but to wait to turn to End Stone. The doomed cries to loved ones could barely be heard over the din of battle.

Gameknight was horrified. Every scream from the condemned warriors hammered a nail of guilt into his soul.

"Come on, we have to go," Monkeypants yelled. "It's time to retreat."

His father pushed the stunned Gameknight999 toward the cobblestone watchtower.

Shaking his head, Gameknight looked at all the NPCs who were losing their lives, and anger bubbled up within his soul. Herobrine had to be stopped, but it wasn't going to happen here.

Gameknight ran for the tunnels that led to the crafting chamber. As planned, archers jumped from the high towers and landed with a splash in shallow pools of water. The last to leave, Hunter finally leapt from the tower and ran to his side.

Glancing over his shoulder, the User-that-is-not-a-user saw a tower of ice appear next to the village's wall. The strange NPC in blue then appeared at the top of the frozen column. Leaping off the wall, he landed on the ground and ran toward the pair. When he drew near, Gameknight realized the stranger was another light-crafter.

As the stranger streaked by, the gates to the village burst open. Zombies and skeletons poured in, the bony white monsters firing a nearly constant flow of arrows. One of the projectiles hit Gameknight in the shoulder, making him cry out in pain. A fleeing villager, hearing the cry, turned and threw a splash potion of healing at him, but completely missed. The glass bottle flew past Gameknight999 and crashed into an approaching zombie. Crying out in pain, the zombie flashed red as the splash potion spread across his decaying body.

Running to the watchtower, the User-that-is-not-a-user watched over his shoulder as the healing potion continued to poison the zombie, finally taking the last of its HP. The monster disappeared with a *pop*, leaving behind three glowing balls of

XP. *That's weird*, Gameknight thought as he ran for the safety of the underground tunnels.

Near the watchtower, Gameknight could see the last of the surviving villagers jumping into holes and disappearing. When he reached the openings, he dropped into one, falling straight down and landing in a shallow pool of water. Realizing he was the last to leave the village, Gameknight quickly filled the water in with stone, stopping any monsters from following.

But this time, the zombies were prepared. One of them poured some water into the hole, creating a liquid stream through which they could descend.

"Oh no," Gameknight said to the villagers heading to the crafting chamber. "They're coming!" he shouted.

But the villagers couldn't move any faster. There were so many of them pressed together and there was only the narrow passage through which to escape. Looking up, the User-that-is-not-a-user could see zombies falling down the watery column, one after another, and more climbing into the flowing liquid. Before Gameknight could draw his sword and get ready for battle, the ice light-crafter appeared at his side.

"It is good to f-f-f-finally meet the User-that-is-not-a-user," the stranger said, flashing an icy smile.

When he plunged his white hands into the water, the liquid immediately froze, changing the waterfall to solid ice. The zombies trapped in the frozen stream flashed with damage, then disappeared as their HP expired. Moving to the other holes filling with water, the light-crafter sealed them all with ice, blocking the monsters from the underground passages.

"That sh-sh-should keep them for a while," the light-crafter stuttered as if he were freezing. "By the way, my . . . my . . . my name is Icebrin."

The pale blue light-crafter extended a white hand that looked as though it were made of snow. Gameknight reached out and took the hand and shook it. Chills ran up his arm as he touched Icebrin's cold fingers.

"I'm grateful for your help," Gameknight said. "But where did you come from?"

"The Oracle thought I might be of assistance in your struggle."

"As always, she was right," Gameknight999 answered.

Suddenly, the column of ice transformed to End Stone as the sparkling transformation wave flowed through the flesh of Minecraft.

"Come on, we need to get out of here!" Gameknight said to his new ally.

He ran down the tunnel, sprinting for the crafting chamber. When he reached the large cavern, he found Monkeypants and Hunter waiting for him impatiently.

"You two have a nice little chat up there?" Hunter asked.

Gameknight looked at her and smiled. His friend's eyes then darted to Icebrin and she reached for an arrow.

"He's a friend sent by the Oracle," the User-that-is-not-a-user explained.

"Perhaps we should get going," Monkeypants said, pointing up to the chamber entrance.

All of them turned to see the transformation wave approaching.

"Come on, let's go," Gameknight said.

Monkeypants grabbed a minecart, as did Hunter, and then Icebrin. As Gameknight watched the wave approach, he looked at the sparkling transformation particles. The purple was like those of the endermen, but there was a pale yellow color to them as well, as though something else was driving the wave, something insipid and sickly. It tickled a memory at the back of his mind but he couldn't quite see it.

"GAMEKNIGHT, HURRY!" a voice shouted from the tunnel.

He placed the metal cart on the tracks and then jumped in. Flipping the lever that activated the TNT, he disappeared into the tunnel as explosions rocketed through the minecart network. While he shot through the darkness, he thought about that strange yellow color he'd seen in the wave. For some reason, he knew it was an important clue . . . but to what?

CHAPTER 23
CRAFTING THE ENDERMEN

The monsters flowed through the desert village like a destructive hurricane. Zombies broke through doors and smashed through empty homes. Skeletons fired arrows at the villagers that had been turned to End Stone; their thirst for destruction making their bows hungry for targets.

One of the zombies knocked over a lit furnace that sat in a newly erected wooden home. Flames licked up the sides of the building and then spread to the ceiling. In seconds, the home was completely engulfed in flame. While searching the other homes not already turned to End Stone, the zombies and skeletons knocked over any furnace that was lit, which caused fire to race through the slowly transforming village, destroying everything wooden. In minutes, a tall column of smoke billowed up into the air; to the monsters, it was a beautiful sight.

Moving out of the village, the monsters clustered on a sandy dune and watched as the wooden structures burned, then turned to stone as the transformation wave flowed across the fiery walls.

As he glided over the defeated village, Herobrine saw his enderman king on a high dune sitting atop his ender-horse, purple teleportation particles hovering nearby. Turning in a sharp arc, the dragon gracefully settled to the ground beside him.

"The battle was well fought," Feyd said as he bowed to the Maker.

"You are a fool," Herobrine growled, his eyes flaring bright. "We lost probably a hundred monsters, most of them zombies and skeletons, of course."

Herobrine glared up at the enderman, his eyes glowing brighter.

"Get off that foolish horse," the dragon commanded.

Quickly, Feyd dismounted, then pushed the horse away. The animal moved near one of the obsidian pillars starting to sprout out of the fresh new End Stone.

"Your endermen are useless in battle," Herobrine stated in a loud grumbling voice. "The skeletons and zombies do all the work while your ridiculous followers just stand back and watch."

"It is not our fault, Maker; it is how we are programmed," Feyd said quickly.

Sensing the danger, he took a step back from the Maker, but the dragon moved closer. Swinging his tail around, Herobrine placed it behind the enderman so that he could not escape.

"We must . . . be directly attacked . . . in order to become enraged so that we can . . . fight," Feyd stammered, his eyes filled with fear.

"Unacceptable," Herobrine said as his dragon-eyes glowed even brighter.

"But we cannot—" Feyd tried to respond but was silenced.

"Be quiet!" the Ender Dragon snapped.

Closing his blazing eyes, Herobrine focused on his shadow-crafting powers. Reaching deep within the lines of AI code that governed his programming, he felt for that familiar pool of energy that enabled him to modify segments of Minecraft's computer code. As he concentrated, he could feel a tingling sensation spread across his clawed hand. His dark talons slowly started to glow a pale sickly yellow, not like the End Stone, which was closer to beige. No, this was a color that had the look of illness and disease to it, as if everything wrong in the world was packed in those glowing claws.

Reaching out with his sharp talons, he plunged them into Feyd's body. Instantly, the king of the endermen went rigid with shock and pain.

"Don't move, if you value your life," Herobrine growled as he closed his eyes and concentrated.

Slowly, the insipid yellow glow oozed into the enderman, making the creature glow all over with the gross color. The enderman opened his toothy mouth as if enraged and in terrible pain, yet at the same time, his eyes glowed bright white with exhilaration and excitement. Yellow light leaked out of his open mouth, casting an eerie glow on the moon-lit desert.

Herobrine opened his eyes and slowly turned his head. Gazing across the desert, he could see all the endermen standing still, their mouths agape like Feyd's. Each glowed with the same sickly illumination, as if a diseased light shone from deep inside. The zombies and skeletons moved away from their shadowy brothers, afraid of what was happening.

Sensing that the job was done, Herobrine withdrew his claws from the king of the endermen and stepped back.

"There. How do you feel now?" Herobrine said, a maniacal grin on the dragon's face.

"What did you do, Maker?" Feyd asked.

A cow moo'ed somewhere out in the darkness. Likely the creature had escaped from the village during the battle. However it got there, Herobrine didn't care. It would not be alive long enough to matter. Flapping his mighty wings, he took to the air and followed the sound.

"Feyd, teleport to that cow," the Maker commanded.

"Why would I—"

"JUST DO IT!" roared the dragon.

Herobrine watched the king of the endermen disappear and then reappear near the docile creature. Settling to the ground, the Ender Dragon looked at the cow, then glanced at Feyd.

"Destroy it," Herobrine commanded.

"You know we cannot attack a creature of the Overworld unless we are provoked," Feyd explained.

Herobrine moved a step closer to the shadowy creature, then spoke in a low, angry voice.

"Destroy the cow before I destroy you."

Fear crept into the enderman's eyes. Balling his hand into a fist, Feyd looked at the cow. As he readied his attack, a mist of sickly yellow particles enveloped the monster. With lightning speed, the king of the endermen attacked the cow, striking it from all directions at once. In seconds, the creature disappeared, leaving behind some glowing balls of XP and a piece of leather.

Staring down at the yellow sparks that danced around his body, Feyd was shocked. When the enderman glanced up at the Maker, Herobrine could see questions tumbling around in the creature's pathetically small mind.

"I changed you," Herobrine said in a loud voice that boomed across the desert. "I changed all the endermen so that you would be useful in my war against the NPCs. Your computer code has been modified so that you can now attack without being provoked. Every enderman is now a lethal weapon—*my* lethal weapon. And in the next battle, I will aim my new weapons at the User-that-is-not-a-user. We will see if he likes my little surprise."

Laughing, Herobrine took to the air, his eyes blazing bright. The sickly yellow glow that had just surrounded the king of the endermen now faded away, leaving him his normal color. Feyd looked again like a shadow in the darkness.

"We will rain destruction down upon the next village and the next and the next, until we have eradicated them all," Herobrine boomed. "And when the last of the NPCs have been turned to End Stone, I will stare Gameknight999 in the eyes and behold his despair. Overcome with grief, completely alone, he will finally take the Gateway of Light back to the physical world, and I will travel there with him."

He flapped his wings and flew higher. To the east, the sun started to rise, the terrain glowing with the orange light of dawn.

"Bring me more monsters!" he yelled. "I want the biggest army ever seen in Minecraft. Every single skeleton, zombie, and enderman from this server must be with me when I face the User-that-is-not-a-user again. When he sees the magnitude of my army, he will cower in fright and beg for mercy."

CHAPTER 24

THE FOG LIFTS

Gameknight was overwhelmed by the bitter taste of failure. The battle in the desert had destroyed a lot of monsters, but the vast number of troops Herobrine still commanded was mind-boggling. They had made just the slightest dent in his machine of destruction at the cost of many NPC lives.

Those poor villagers had expected the User-that-is-not-a-user to keep them safe, Gameknight thought. *And instead, I got them killed . . .*

Every fiber in his soul screamed at him: FAILURE!

He had to do something fast to defeat Herobrine and his army of monsters, but everything he'd tried hadn't worked. Gameknight was so frustrated, he could hardly think.

"I hate this responsibility. How can I do this?" he said to the dark minecart tunnel. "I'm so afraid to fail that I'm now afraid to try."

The images of villagers turned to End Stone played through his mind. Nothing he tried seemed to stop the flow of monsters and End Stone. First, it had just been the endermen, and then the zombies, and now skeletons. *Where will it end?*

He knew the answer to that question deep down in his soul: it would end at Crafter's village. That would be the place where the NPCs of the Overworld had to stop Herobrine and his monster army. If they failed there, then Minecraft was doomed. The Council of Crafters would have no choice but to disconnect them from the Source.

But if they managed to stop Herobrine's monster army, the transformation wave would still be out there, moving across the landscape, destroying all life. Stopping the monsters was not enough; they must also stop that transformation wave.

Closing his eyes, he thought about that terrible wave. He could see Herobrine spitting that terrible poison onto the ground, starting the wave, but as it flowed across the land, something had to be giving it energy to continue its terrible purpose. Those sparks along the edge, purple and pale yellow . . .

"Wait a minute," Gameknight exclaimed aloud to the darkness. "The pale yellow sparks are the same as those that surround Herobrine. They were the sign of his crafting."

He knew Herobrine's powers took on that sickly yellow color; he'd seen it many times before. But when that wave moved across the surface of Minecraft, it had the same sparkling color. Suddenly, Gameknight realized what was keeping that wave moving across the land.

"It's Herobrine's crafting powers!" Gameknight shouted, his voice echoing down the tunnel.

From the darkness, he could hear his father shouting something, but he was too far away.

"Herobrine must be the source," he murmured softly.

The music of Minecraft swelled, filling the tunnel with melodic tones and harmonious sounds. It was the Oracle; she was confirming his realization.

"Herobrine is the source, isn't he?" Gameknight asked the Oracle, his voice echoing off the stone walls. "If we destroy the source, then the transformation wave will stop, is that correct?"

The music of Minecraft grew even louder.

"That's it!"

Suddenly, Gameknight knew what he had to do to stop that terrible transformation wave: he had to destroy Herobrine. They didn't need to stop the monsters, for there would always be more coming at them from the darkness. It was Herobrine who had to be stopped.

But how?

Gameknight knew that Herobrine would spit his purple poison onto the Overworld as soon as he felt his monsters were in trouble. He'd done it twice now and he'd do it again.

Another piece of the solution fell into place: the obsidian.

"Yes, of course, but how do we get him close enough for us to attack him?"

More and more parts of the puzzle emerged through the evaporating fog of fear that had clouded his mind for so long. Gameknight experienced a sudden burst of confidence. His father had been right; focusing on the fear only made things seem worse. But focusing his attention on something else, anything else, allowed him to think clearly.

Ideas rushed at him from all sides. Images of the battlefields formed in his head, where they would put the traps, and how they would ensnare the dragon.

"Water—we'll use water, and dispensers, hundreds of them," he said. "Surprise will be our ally."

But would the villagers trust this crazy plan?

CHAPTER 25

GAMEKNIGHT'S SONG

When Gameknight's minecart pulled into Crafter's village, he found what he expected: panic.

"The dragon turned my dear Woodcutter to End Stone," someone shouted.

"He destroyed Builder . . ."

"And Cobbler . . ."

"And Carver . . ."

The villagers were terrified. The dragon had spit his vile poison directly on the NPCs and instantly tore their lives from them, leaving behind a stone mockery of what they had once been. It was enraging and horrifying, something beyond belief.

Looking across the crafting chamber, Gameknight could see Crafter trying to calm the villagers' fears, but he was just one small voice of reason trying to hold back a flood of uncertainty. Moving to his side, Gameknight spoke into the young NPC's ear.

"Give me one of your fireworks."

"What?" Crafter asked. "I hardly think this is the time to—"

"Just give me one!" Gameknight snapped.

Crafter looked confused, but handed him one of the rockets. Gameknight took it and gave him a smile, then leapt up into the air as he placed a block of stone under his feet. Jumping three more times, Gameknight stood high over all the NPCs' heads, but this still did not quiet the crowd.

Leaning out, he placed a block of cobblestone on the side of the column on which he stood, then planted the rocket on the ground. It shot up into the air and exploded with a mighty *BANG!* high overhead. The green sparkling face of a creeper stared down at the frightened NPCs.

"You can choose to listen and survive or panic and die!" Gameknight shouted.

That got their attention; the NPCs turned to face him.

"But all those monsters . . ."

"And Herobrine . . ."

"Yes, yes, I know all about that," Gameknight replied. "I was there, remember? Herobrine and his army are still coming, but we did what we set out to do: delay them so that we could prepare our defenses. Where's Digger?"

"Here," a deep voice boomed from across the chamber.

The stocky NPC pushed through the crush of people to stand at Gameknight's side. Herder, who was covered with sweat and dirt from his labors, followed close behind.

"Are the defenses ready?" Gameknight asked.

"We did as Shawny instructed," Digger replied. "I think we will have many new surprises in store for Herobrine and his monsters."

"Excellent," Gameknight said, "but I have a few more things that need to be built." He scanned the crowd for the light-crafters and found the three of them huddled in the corner of the chamber. "I will need you three for something special. We're going to build a net to catch us an annoying dragon."

The light-crafters looked up at Gameknight and smiled.

"And where is Morgana?" Gameknight asked. "We will need many of the witch's potions before the day is through. Where is she?"

"The witch fled as soon as she heard about Herobrine and his monsters," someone shouted.

"I didn't flee," came a scratchy voice from the chamber entrance. "I went to the Nether for Nether Wart and glowstone dust. As soon as I heard Herobrine had an army of zombies, I knew what would be needed."

"Potions of healing," Gameknight said, nodding to the old woman.

"Exactly," Morgana said, a wry smile flowing across her wrinkled face. "I have them brewing as we speak."

"Perfect," Gameknight said. "We'll have need for many splash potions, but I need something else from you, as well."

One side of the witch's unibrow raised, a curious look on her face.

"We'll need splash water bottles," Gameknight said. "I want them for—"

"No need to explain, User-that-is-not-a-user," the witch said. "Your intent is obvious. I'll get started on it."

Before Gameknight could say anything else, the aged NPC turned and headed back to Gameknight's castle and her brewing lab.

"How are a few potions going to help us against Herobrine's transformation wave?" one of the new

NPCs asked. "I saw what it did to my village and my friends. You aren't going to heal them with some Nether Wart and melon."

"You're right," Gameknight said. "I don't know how to heal those who have been transformed, but I do know how to prevent the transformation from happening ever again."

The crafting chamber became deathly silent. Gameknight gazed across the sea of faces below him, making sure they could see the determination on his face.

"My father used to tell me something that I did not understand until recently," Gameknight explained. "He told me that I was focusing too much on my fear, for I am terrified of failing all of you. I'm afraid that I might not be smart enough or strong enough to defeat Herobrine. The more I thought about my fear, the stronger its hold was on my mind, until I couldn't even think. You see, I didn't understand what my real strength was, what my song was." He looked at his father and smiled. "And after what felt like a defeat in the last battle, I did some hard thinking in the minecart tunnels, and I finally realized what my talent is. And although I still think I'm usually good at it, it's not griefing."

The silence in the chamber was deafening. Gameknight could hear his pulse pounding in his ears, his heart beating with every CPU clock tick.

"You see, my talent is refusing to accept defeat. Even though I'm afraid of Herobrine and his mob, I will not be intimidated and terrorized. It reminds me too much of the bullies back at my school. I've been afraid for too long and I refuse to cower any longer. And as soon as I stopped focusing on my fears, the solutions appeared in my head with crystal clarity."

"What must we do to stop the transformation wave?" one of the NPCs asked.

"The transformation wave has to get its energy from somewhere, for nothing comes for free in Minecraft. There must be a source for the code that drives that terrible wave. The grass gets the code to grow from the sun and water. The apples get their code from the trees, wool from the sheep, fish from the streams. . . . Everything is interconnected. All we need do is find the source for that tide of transformation and then seal it up like blocking a water source to stop a raging river." Gameknight paused for a moment to let this sink in, then continued. "Destroy the source and we destroy the wave."

"What is the source?" someone asked from behind him.

Turning, he found it was Crafter who had spoken, his big blue eyes filled with questions.

"Herobrine himself," Gameknight said.

This caused a flurry of questions to erupt all at once. Gameknight held up his hand and brought the chamber back into order.

"Herobrine created the transformation wave with his evil crafting powers," the User-that-is-not-a-user said. "The fact that the sparkling yellow particles are in both the wave and around Herobrine himself tells me that this is true. Those particles drive both of their behaviors, and if we eliminate those sickly yellow sparks, then we will stop both of these threats. And to do this, we must destroy the dragon. Herobrine is our target; the monsters are just a distraction, but we must destroy that distraction so that the Ender Dragon will commit himself to the battle. The destruction of the monster army will draw Herobrine into our trap. I should have realized this a long time ago, but my fear clouded my vision. It took a lesson from a monkey in a superman outfit to clarify it for me."

Some of the villagers laughed as they looked at Monkeypants, then brought their eyes back to Gameknight999.

"With the help of our light-crafter friends and the new defenses designed by Shawny, we will have a few surprises in store for the Ender Dragon," Gameknight said. "But I can't do this by myself. I'll need every able-bodied NPC to help in order for this to work. The question that really needs to be answered is: are you still with me? But before you answer, know that I will ask you all to do something difficult—no, terrifying. In fact, I'm scared just thinking about it, but it will be the surprise that will shift the balance of power in this war. I'm asking you to stand at my side and stare straight into what you will think is certain death—and not flinch. So I ask you: will you stand up against Herobrine at my side? For without all of you, we are doomed. Will you stand with me?"

The NPCs looked at each other while they considered the overwhelming danger. As they looked at each other, the unwelcome feeling of fear began to grow within the User-that-is-not-a-user as thunderous silence filled the chamber.

They don't trust me. I'm all alone.

Gameknight hung his head and stared at his feet, the feeling of failure washing over him like a tidal wave. Thoughts of everything he'd done wrong surged through his mind: the people he'd failed, the deaths he'd caused . . .

Thump . . . thump . . . thump . . . thump . . .

A rhymthical sound began to fill the chamber. It echoed at the back of Gameknight's mind, but his thoughts were elsewhere, his eyes glued to his diamond coated feet.

Thump . . . Thump . . . Thump . . . Thump . . .

Maybe if he could defeat Herobrine on his own, then the villagers would trust him again . . . but he was just a kid. How was he going to do that?

THUMP . . . THUMP . . . THUMP . . . THUMP . . .

The percussive beat was now like thunder in the crafting chamber, the beats echoing off the wall and creating a pattern of metallic bang followed by a softer thumpy echo.

Gameknight looked up and found all the NPCs staring at him, their eyes fixed with determination. Each had their weapons out and were banging them on their chests, creating a cacophony of crashes and thuds, smiles on all the square faces. And at that moment, for the first time since this adventure started, Gameknight999 actually thought they might have a chance.

CHAPTER 26

THE HUNTER FINDS HIS PREY

Herobrine materialized high above the clouds in a forest biome. Behind him, the forest spread out, covering the rolling hills and plateaus, the pine trees looking tiny from this height. In front of him, the forest abruptly ended, giving way to a grassy plains biome. Looking down, he could tell that his enderman scout was correct: it was right where he said it would be—the village of that boy-crafter. He could somehow feel the presence of his enemy in the distant village and had to resist the urge to attack.

"I should have realized he'd come back here," Herobrine said to himself. "The User-that-is-not-a-user lacks any creativity."

Flapping his mighty wings, he turned and flew away from the village until it was just on the edge of visibility. Staring down, Herobrine could still remember when he'd battled Gameknight999 right out there in front of that walled village. The User-that-is-not-a-user had been narrowly saved by a pack of wild wolves, probably sent by that old hag, the Oracle.

"You don't have the Oracle here to save you anymore, do you Gameknight999?" the dragon growled.

He could feel his eyes growing bright with hatred and quickly pushed aside his violent thoughts. The Ender Dragon didn't want to give away his presence, not yet. Turning in a graceful arch, Herobrine flew away from his prey, then slowly descended. Settling to the ground in a clearing of white and red flowers, the Maker motioned for his scout to come to his side.

"You are right, the User-that-is-not-a-user is in that village," Herobrine said. "Go back to the army and have the endermen teleport all monsters to this clearing. We will use the cover of this forest to sneak up on them and take them by surprise. This time, it will be Herobrine who has a surprise for the NPCs."

The enderman chuckled, then disappeared in a cloud of purple and yellow particles.

Smiling, the dragon reached down and plucked a red flower from the ground. Holding the delicate plant up to his eyes, Herobrine let the smallest drop of purple poison drip onto one of the petals. Instantly, the flower began to change to End Stone as a wave of lavender and pale yellow sparks flowed across the plant. In an instant, the red flower was now End Stone, and the pale petals looked petrified and lifeless. Clenching his taloned fist, Herobrine crushed the dead flower and let the pale remains litter the ground.

"Soon that will be *you* crumbling within my grasp, Gameknight999," the dragon said with a vile, demonic laugh.

CHAPTER 27

LET IT BEGIN

Gameknight999 stood on the fortified wall of his castle, looking across the beautiful landscape. This would soon become the scene of terrible destruction, he thought grimly. They had prepared everything as per Shawny's instructions. Instead of just a series of walls, archer towers, and TNT bombs, like Herobrine was expecting, Shawny had orchestrated a battle plan that would move the enemy through the battlefield until they were right where Gameknight wanted them.

"Those skilled in war bring the enemy to the field of battle and are not brought there by him," Gameknight mumbled to himself. It was one of the many quotes from the sixth-century Chinese strategist Sun Tzu that his social studies teacher, Mr. Planck, had posted on his wall of fame.

"What did you say, son?" Monkeypants asked.

"Nothing, I was just thinking aloud," Gameknight replied. "Are all the villagers ready?"

"Yes, they are ready . . . and scared."

"Do you think they'll do what I've asked, or will they run?" Gameknight asked his father.

"I don't know," Monkeypants271 replied. "You've asked them to do something incredibly dangerous."

Turning from his father, the User-that-is-not-a-user surveyed the battlefield. A series of minecart tracks shot out in all directions, many of them powered and glowing red. Redstone torches decorated the area, each lighting different sections of track. Mixed with the green grass, it almost looked like some kind of strange red-green Christmas scene. The thought made Gameknight smile.

Interspersed throughout the landscape, he could just barely see the many gray dispensers. They stood out like metallic punctuation marks on the darkening landscape, each positioned at the end of a silent redstone trace. Repeaters broke the lines of ruby-colored dust, the white squares and silent torches looked eager to fulfill their task. They would get the chance soon enough.

"What I don't understand, son, is this: won't Herobrine see all of your preparations?" Monkeypants asked.

"Yes, he will."

"So won't he know that we have traps set for his monsters?"

"Of course he will," Gameknight replied. "But he doesn't care about the lives of anything or anyone other than himself. He will sacrifice a small group of monsters as a test, but when he thinks he has us trapped and cornered, he'll commit all of his forces in a massive attack and try to wipe us out in a single stroke."

"That sounds like a bad thing," his father said, worry in his voice.

"Normally it would be, but we aren't going to show him everything—only what we want him to see." Gameknight turned and faced his father. "Our whole plan depends on making Herobrine come to us and commit himself to the battle. If he stays out of arm's reach, then all is lost."

"You think you can get him to join the battle?"

"I have something that he wants more than anything," the User-that-is-not-a-user said.

"Oh really, what is that?" his father asked.

Gameknight sighed. "Me."

"I don't really like the sound of that," Monkey-pants said.

"I know, but—"

A rocket streaked up into the air, exploding in a shower of orange and yellow sparks. It was followed by another rocket off to the left, and then another to the right.

"They're here," Gameknight said softly.

Looking up to the dark obsidian tower that loomed high over the central keep, Gameknight drew his diamond sword and waved it in the air. Instantly, someone unrolled a long red banner, the cloth fluttering in the gentle breeze that always blew from east to west. Warriors ran up to the fortified walls, both around his castle and in the village that sat nearby. Arrows were notched to bows as NPCs crouched behind rocky crenellations, ready for the hail of arrows sure to come.

They could hear them approaching.

A morose wail drifted out of the forest. It was a sad, hopeless sound from creatures that had forgotten the wondrous beauty of life and could now only know suffering and despair. Accompanying it were the percussive rattles of bone on bone. The grinding and clattering of bleach-white body parts echoed across the rolling grass-covered plain like a million strained castanets.

In the distance, Gameknight could see a large group of monsters slowly push through the oak trees and approach the battlefield. When they saw the fortified walls, the zombie moans turned to angry growls. They glared at the defenders through the darkness. Gameknight wished they would just start the attack and charge, but the zombies and skeletons stayed far from the village and castle, having learned their lesson.

Not a problem, Gameknight thought. *We'll coax them forward soon enough.*

Suddenly, a pair of white dots could be seen moving through the sky, banking this way and that. Glancing at the pinpoints, the User-that-is-not-a-user watched as Herobrine approached, materializing out of the darkness and settling to the ground amidst the forest. Swinging his heavy spiked tail, he knocked down trees like they were blades of grass, carving out a clearing from which he could watch the battle.

"I have come for you, Gameknight999!" the dragon roared. "I will leave this village in shattered ruins, as I have done to all the others. No mercy will be given to anyone who opposes us." The dragon glared at the defenders, his eyes glowing bright white. "Drop your weapons now and come out from behind your pathetic walls, and I may spare your lives."

"You bore me with your constant chatter," Gameknight shouted.

The NPCs laughed, making Herobrine's eyes glow even brighter with hatred.

Just then, the monster kings emerged from behind the dragon as more of the army approached.

Now there was a constant line of creatures wrapping around three sides of the village and castle, their green and white and black bodies creating a kaleidoscope of evil.

Gameknight was shocked at the numbers that stood before him. There must have been five hundred monsters out there, maybe a thousand. As he glanced around at the other NPCs, Gameknight took in their fearful faces as they tried to count the opposing force.

"Their numbers are meaningless," Gameknight shouted. "Stick to the plan and stay strong. This is the day we take back the Overworld and drive the monsters into the shadows."

He expected cheers, but heard nothing—just terrified silence.

And then a maniacal chuckle drifted across the landscape. Turning to face the sound, Gameknight could see Feyd sitting atop his ender-horse, his body shrouded in both purple and yellow particles.

Why yellow particles? Gameknight thought.

The vile enderman had a look of malicious glee on his face as he gestured to one of his subordinates. Stepping around the ender-horse, a pair of zombies carried what looked like a statue.

"It sounds as though your friends lack faith in you, Loser-that-is-a-loser," Feyd screeched. "I am not surprised. They are finally coming to the conclusion that you are nothing but a coward. Your failure to lead these villagers has caused the death of many. So, out of the kindness of my heart, I am returning one of your pathetic NPCs to you."

Waving a long dark red arm, the king of the endermen motioned that the zombies move out in front of the army holding the petrified villager high in the air. Gameknight could see that it was one of the many NPCs who had fallen victim to the transformation wave.

"Return this statue to his leader," Feyd commanded from his dark horse.

The two zombies looked at Xa-Tul. The zombie king nodded his head, and the two monsters threw the statue high into the air. It crashed to the ground, splintering into a million pieces. Feyd then urged his horse forward and his steed stomped on any of the pieces still recognizable, until all that was left was dust.

The villagers yelled and screamed at the monster. That atrocity had transformed their fear into rage, and now all of the NPCs wanted the monsters to come. Some drew back arrows and fired, but the monsters were still out of range.

"Hold your fire!" Gameknight shouted. "You will all have your opportunity to take revenge. Just stick to the plan and stay strong."

Glancing around at the warriors throughout the castle, Gameknight could see looks of unbridled hate focused toward the monster army. The uncertainty and fear that had been there moments before was completely gone, blasted away by that act of senseless violence.

He smiled as he turned back toward Herobrine and the monster kings.

"Herobrine and your vile kings, I forbid you from entering this village," the User-that-is-not-a-user shouted. "And what's more, I forbid you from leaving this battlefield. This will be the place of your destruction."

Turning, he looked down at an NPC who was standing before a wall covered with buttons and levers. Gameknight nodded and said a single word to him: "Red."

The NPC smiled, then reached up and flipped a series of levers.

"May the fates of war smile down upon us," Gameknight999 said. "Let it begin."

CHAPTER 28

THE HUNTERS BECOME THE HUNTED

Gameknight looked out across the battlefield and imagined he could see the redstone signal slowly moving through the underground tunnels. The villagers had carefully laid out these crimson traces as per Shawny's battle plans, and now they were coming to life. All the NPCs held their breaths as they waited for something to happen, the tension visible on their boxy faces.

Staring out at the monster horde, the User-that-is-not-a-user could see the many tall fence posts that had been placed throughout the area, each with a different color banner hanging from their peak. The monster horde had stopped in the red zone.

Perfect, Gameknight thought.

Suddenly, explosions tore into the landscape as hidden TNT burst into life ten blocks behind the monsters. Gameknight watched as Herobrine leapt into the air, beating his massive leathery wings to gain altitude. Feyd turned and looked back at the explosions, then glanced at the User-that-is-not-a-user and smiled. Just as the monster was about to say something, more explosions punctuated the landscape, this time a little closer to the monster army.

"The Fool has missed his target twice!" boomed Xa-Tul. "The zombies will enjoy tearing this village apart when—"

Just then the explosions tore into the back ranks of the monsters, driving them forward in a panic. Gameknight smiled as the zombies, endermen, and skeletons scurried forward, their monstrous faces glancing nervously over their shoulders as more blocks of TNT detonated beneath their feet.

The NPCs cheered.

The monsters continued to move forward, the zombies, skeletons, and endermen shuffling past the dispensers that were distributed throughout the battlefield, eager to escape the explosions that blossomed at their rear. Gameknight could tell the monsters expected something to come out of the metallic cubes, but the dark opening of the dispensers were still; it was not yet time for them.

As the monsters moved closer, the archers started firing. Instantly, hundreds of skeletons returned fire, sending back twenty arrows for each one fired by a villager. As the incoming projectiles sailed through the air, Gameknight signaled to the tall watchtower at the center of his castle, waving with his iron sword. An NPC removed the red banner and hung a yellow one in its place. Instantly, the villagers crouched behind stone barriers and placed cubes of cobblestone up and over their heads, shielding them from the pointed rain that fell down upon them.

The skeletons fired as quickly as their bony hands could draw back arrows. Gameknight ducked behind a block of obsidian to avoid the deadly rain then signaled to those NPCs standing next to the minecart tracks that pierced the dark walls of the castle and rocky walls of the village. As one, the NPCs placed TNT carts on the tracks and gave them a shove. When they reached the powered rails, the carts shot forward, heading toward the skeletons. Just before the end of the tracks, the carts ran over an activator rail, causing the TNT to begin blinking. Gameknight smiled as the carts exploded amidst the skeletons, blasting HP into nothing.

Not waiting for instructions, the villagers continued to place TNT minecarts on the tracks, sending them into the field. As they rolled forward, NPCs flipped levers, changing where the carts would go, sending the rolling explosives to a different destination each time.

The monsters, not knowing what to do, scattered, allowing the NPC archers to move out behind their protective barriers and open fire.

Some of the monsters tried to retreat, but Shawny had expected this. Gameknight flicked a glance to the NPC in front of the control board, who pressed more levers and caused explosions to reverberate across the landscape. With nowhere else to go, the monsters had no choice but to move forward, closer to the castle and village walls.

Glancing down at the monsters, Gameknight could see their explosions were thinning out the monster horde. With the skeletons and zombies being relatively slow, they were taking the brunt of the damage, their numbers having been cut in half.

But the endermen, using their teleportation powers, were able to quickly escape the rolling bombs and remain relatively unscathed. None of the archers dared fire at the dark creatures and risk enraging them, leaving them relatively unharmed, for now. Some of the dark creatures were moving backward, hoping to escape the carnage, but Gameknight would not allow that.

"Activate the first dispensers," the User-that-is-not-a-user yelled.

More levers were flipped. Underground, redstone circuits activated, sending signals to the dispensers, each one holding a single bucket of water. As the liquid spilled outward, a block of TNT exploded under the dispenser, creating wide craters in the ground that the water quickly filled. In an instant, a circle of water twelve blocks wide and as many deep surrounded the village and castle on all sides.

"Go to the next ones," Gameknight shouted as he stared at the dark monsters.

More water flowed across the landscape, covering the ground with the thing deadly to all endermen. With their escape blocked and explosions still tearing away at the ground around them, the monsters were forced to move even closer.

"OPEN THE GATES!" the User-that-is-not-a-user shouted.

Slowly, the doors to the castle and village creaked open, giving the monsters access to the interior. But the monsters did not take the bait.

"More minecarts!" Gameknight screamed. "Send them all out!"

A constant flow of rolling bombs moved out onto the battlefield. The blinking minecarts crashed into the monsters and came to life. The explosions tore great holes into the enemy formations. The monsters' numbers fell as the TNT took its toll.

"Activate all the dispensers outside the walls!" Gameknight shouted. "Everyone to your positions."

The NPC at the control board flipped all of the levers, then ran to the walls. Watching the village, Gameknight could see everyone following suite, moving away from the open area of the village and hiding behind protective structures against the walls.

Suddenly, the land outside the walls erupted with watery explosions as the dispensers disgorged their contents, then disappeared as the block of TNT hidden underground burst into life. The battlefield was now covered with water and craters. Many of the zombies and skeletons survived the blasts, but the endermen took serious damage from all the water. With no place else to run, the endermen teleported into the castle and village. As they materialized, a mist of purple particles surrounded the terrible monsters. Glaring at the villagers surrounding them, the lavender sparks quickly turned to a sickly yellow and the monsters did the unexpected: they attacked.

"They're attacking!" one of the NPCs yelled.

Some of the endermen charged toward NPCs, slamming into the villagers with lightning fast blows. The villagers slashed at the endermen, careful to stay near the walls. As usual, the dark creatures teleported away when they saw blades streaking toward them.

"How can that be?" yelled another.

The endermen all chuckled eerily. It caused tiny square goosebumps to form on arms and necks.

Gameknight held up his hands as he looked down on the monsters.

"You are not welcome here, you never have been, and you never will be!" Gameknight shouted.

The dark creatures' eyes glowed white with rage, and the yellow particles grew brighter. They stared up at Gameknight with venomous hatred. But just before they attacked, the User-that-is-not-a-user smiled, then flipped a lever that sat on the block next to him.

CHAPTER 29

FACING THE ENDERMEN

R edstone circuits suddenly came to life. Bright red lines lit the top of the fortified walls, repeaters glowing bright all around the castle and village. Instantly, the dispensers that pointed inward toward the center of the village came to life and belched out their contents, firing a nearly constant stream of splash bottles, each filled with water. At the same time, dispensers facing outward from the walls started firing splash potions of healing down upon the struggling monsters.

The water covered the endermen, causing their skin to sizzle and smoke as they flashed red with damage. Teleporting from place to place, the shadowy monsters tried to avoid the fragile glass bottles, but the deadly dispensers had the entire courtyard covered with their overlapping fields of fire. They had nowhere to hide.

Outside the walls, the healing potions were having the opposite effect, as they were intended for NPCs. The medicinal liquid, though beneficial to villagers, was deadly to the zombies. The splash potions rained down upon the green creatures, causing them to flashed red with damage as their HP was slowly consumed.

"Archers, open fire on the endermen and the skeletons," Gameknight shouted.

Signaling to the NPC high up in the watch-tower, the User-that-is-not-a-user crossed both his swords over his head and a blue banner draped out the window above him. The archers saw the flag and turned their pointed barbs upon the endermen and skeletons.

Firing as one, half the NPCs loosed volley after volley of arrows down upon the endermen from the fortified walls, while the other half focused their attack upon the bony creatures struggling through the watery pits outside. The endermen flashed red as they teleported about the courtyard, but it did not help. Arrows still found dark bodies as hundreds of pointed shafts fell down upon the monsters.

One of the dark monsters teleported to the top of the wall to escape the hail of arrows and water and charged toward Gameknight999. With his swords already drawn, the User-that-is-not-a-user blocked a dark fist as it shot toward his head. Jumping high into the air, he struck down on the creature with both swords, but the monster teleported behind him. Before the monster could attack, Monkey-pants was there with his own blade, tearing into the monster's HP until it disappeared.

Looking across the castle courtyard, Game-knight could see more endermen vying for the safety of the catwalks, only to meet sharp blades when they materialized. Glancing at the village, Gameknight could see Crafter on the fortified walls, directing the battle. They, too, had ender-men within the walls, but now the ground inside the village was covered with as much water as was beyond the walls. The endermen had no place to run. Some tried to teleport to the tops of the village homes, but the onslaught of arrows from the ring of archers around them soon wore them down to nothing. After five minutes of intense fighting, the last of the endermen were gone.

Outside the walls, the skeletons were faring better, as they could fight back, but it wasn't the plan to destroy them, just keep them busy. The monsters fired up at the NPCs, forcing the villagers to hide behind blocks of cobblestone. Peeking out behind the blocks, the archers fired into the collection of monsters, not even bothering to aim.

Zombies were mixed in with the skeletons. With the constant rain of healing potions, the monsters flashed almost continuously as their HP evaporated. Eventually, the last of the zombies perished, leaving only the skeletons behind.

Glancing to the village, Gameknight could see there were at least two hundred of the pale white creatures firing back up at the fortified walls, and at least a hundred in front of his castle. They would not be able to trade arrow for arrow with these creatures; it would be too costly to his friends. But he had anticipated this situation and gestured to the light-crafters standing near the entrance.

"Icebrin, now!" Gameknight yelled.

The strange light-crafter stepped out of the gates and plunged his hands into the flowing waters that now surrounded the castle and village. Instantly, the water turned to ice, releasing the skeletons from the slowing currents, but also freeing up the villagers, as well.

Looking up to the watchtower, Gameknight signaled with his diamond sword straight up, and his iron sword out to the side. A white banner came out of the window, replacing the blue. NPCs responded, pulling horses out of sheltered corrals, and mounting their steeds with swords drawn and armor shining bright. Glancing to the village, he could see Crafter waving his own sword high over his head; they were ready. Turning to the NPC in the watchtower, Gameknight raised his iron sword so that both swords pointed skyward. The white banner was replaced with an orange one, signaling the charge.

The ground shook with thunder as a hundred warriors rode out of the castle, the same number leaving the village. With the water frozen, the horses were able to move quickly toward the monsters. The skeletons turned and fired upon the advancing cavalry, scoring many hits and leaving horses riderless, but as soon as the warriors closed the distance, the bows were no match for blades. Tearing through the formations, the warriors struck hard and fast, causing skeletons to flash red with damage as their HP was consumed.

Gameknight wanted to be out there leading the charge, but he knew his place was here, orchestrating the attack. He wished they had the legendary Smithy of the Two Swords with them, a courageous leader from the first great zombie invasion that he'd heard so much about. With Smithy out there leading that charge, maybe more of the horses would still have riders.

But he knew he had to stay in the castle, for this wasn't even the real attack. Gameknight knew that the Last Battle was far from over, and he shook with fear when he thought about what still stood between them and victory.

After three passes of the cavalry through the skeleton formations, the bony white monsters were gone. Gameknight could see Digger leading the charge, mopping up the last of the skeletons.

They'd won.

A cheer sprang up across the landscape as the NPCs yelled with jubilation. Gameknight glanced across the battlefield and thought it almost looked beautiful; hundreds of glowing balls of XP floated all across the plain like sparkling lights, each one shining bright with color. But then he noticed the piles of armor and swords that lay on the ground near the bones and zombie flesh. There had been a cost to this victory and it had been dear. And this was just the first wave.

Looking up at the watchtower, Gameknight held both swords straight out from his sides. The NPC nodded and placed a green banner on the wall.

Instantly, shouts rang out from the fortified walls, calling the cavalry back to safety. Instead of riding back into the enclosures, the warriors dismounted and ran back to the castle, slapping their horses on the rump to send them running away, the cavalry near the village doing the same.

Watching those in the village, Gameknight could see the NPCs all running for a set of wide stairs leading underground. They disappeared into the darkness of the tunnel, running as fast as they could. At the same time, the villagers within the castle sprinted for the large keep that stood at its center. With weapons in hand, the defenders vanished behind a set of iron doors. Gameknight knew the NPCs from the village would emerge from the underground tunnel and would soon be safely within the keep as well, leaving only Gameknight999, Monkeypants271, and the light-crafters standing on the fortified obsidian wall.

"When will it happen?" Monkeypants asked.

"Soon," Gameknight replied.

"Are you sssure he's goinggg to do wwwhat you expect?" Grassbrin asked in his sing-song voice.

"I don't know," Gameknight answered. "If he doesn't do what we've planned for, then we might still lose this war."

"Grafapted, Gameknight," Treebrin grumbled.

Gameknight looked at Grassbrin, confused.

"He sssaid 'Have faith, Gameknight,' which I thinnnk is good advissse," Grassbrin replied.

"All we can do is wait and see what happens," Monkeypants said.

Suddenly, an ear splitting roar erupted from the forest. Glancing toward the sound, Gameknight could see Herobrine's hulking body smash through the trees as if they were just sticks, his eyes blazing with hatred, their gaze fixed directly on the User-that-is-not-a-user. And as the monster raised its massive head up high, Gameknight999 shook with fear.

CHAPTER 30
A FRIEND'S FATE

The dragon slowly settled to the ground outside of arrow range. Moving up next to him, Xa-Tul and Reaper glared up at Gameknight999.

"This is not over, Fool!" the zombie king yelled.

"You're right, it's not over yet," Gameknight replied. "You three are still alive, and you must still be punished for your crimes against Minecraft."

"There are more than three here," screeched a voice from behind the dragon.

Slowly, Feyd rode around Herobrine and moved to the Maker's side. Behind him walked at least a hundred endermen, all of them sparkling with sickly yellow sparks.

"M-m-more endermen?" stuttered Icebrin, his voice filled with trepidation.

"The endermen are a distraction," Gameknight said, trying to sound confident as his voice cracked with fear. "Focus on the plan."

Taking in a deep breath, the User-that-is-not-a-user turned to Icebrin and nodded. The light-crafter slid down a ladder to the ground level, then moved outside and plunged his chilly hands into the ice that covered the landscape. Instantly, the ice turned to flowing water again, the liquid barrier impassable by the shadowy creatures.

"If you think that will do any good, you are as stupid as you are foolish," Herobrine boomed.

Gameknight said nothing. Sliding down the ladder himself, he moved to the iron doors and waited for Icebrin to come back into the castle. Once he was inside, Gameknight closed the doors, then moved to a nearby block of obsidian next to the wall and stood there. Looking up at his father and the light-crafters, he motioned them to come down from the fortified wall and stand on other blocks of obsidian.

"Quickly," Gameknight999 said. "Get to your blocks."

His father and the light-crafters each chose a dark block and stood on top of it. Now all of them stood next to the obsidian wall that surrounded the castle, well hidden under the raised walkway that ringed the courtyard.

"Now we wait," Gameknight said.

Glancing through the iron bars that had been placed in the dark wall, Gameknight looked at the dragon and monster kings. The endermen just stood there, unable to approach because of all the water that flowed around the castle, their bodies bathed in sickly yellow embers, ready to attack.

Releasing a loud guttural growl, Herobrine flapped his huge wings and shot into the air. Flying in a great circle, he flew around the castle and village, looking for more traps. Gameknight knew he would see none.

Swooping down to the village, the dragon flew directly toward the fortified cobblestone wall.

Picking up speed, Herobrine smashed into the cobblestone, shattering the barricade and making the interior now accessible. Banking in a sharp curve, the dragon then flew toward the Gameknight's castle. Diving straight toward the dark wall, the dragon smashed into the fortifications, but did no damage—the flying reptile just bouncing off the dark purple-black wall. Turning, the dragon tried it again, whipping his tail so that it crashed into the obsidian barrier, and again, the battlements remained unchanged. With a growl, Herobrine flew back up into the sky.

"Why can't he break through?" Monkeypants asked.

"Anyone who has gone to The End and fought the dragon knows that nothing from the Overworld can survive the dragon's touch," Gameknight explained. "But obsidian is End material; the dragon cannot break it."

Monkeypants nodded then smiled, pride flashing across his silly monkey-face.

"Leave us alone," croaked a voice from the keep.

Gameknight could see Farmer running out of the rectangular structure and toward the castle gates.

"No, get back!" Gameknight yelled, but the old woman ignored him.

Stitcher sprinted after her, but the young girl had clearly been surprised by the elderly NPC's speed, for the old woman was almost to the castle wall before Stitcher made it out of the keep.

Gameknight looked at Stitcher and readied a charge toward the old woman, but the young NPC raised a hand and stopped him.

"Concentrate on the battle, Gameknight," Stitcher yelled. "I'll get Farmer."

Fear pulsed through his veins as he watched the bizarre race.

When Farmer reached the castle wall, she pressed the button, causing the iron doors to swing open. Drawing an iron sword from her inventory, the old woman waded out into the flowing waters.

"You leave our village alone!" she screamed in a scratchy voice.

Peering through the iron bars, Gameknight scanned the skies, frantically looking for the monster that he knew was somewhere overhead. Suddenly, a ferocious roar split the air like titanic thunder. Streaking across the battlefield, the Ender Dragon soared down to the ground, pulling up at the last instant and gliding ominously a few blocks above the churning waters that surrounded the village and castle. As he flew, Herobrine spit his venomous purple poison onto the ground.

"Oh no," Gameknight said.

Stitcher shot through the doors and grabbed the old woman. Knocking the sword from her hand, she pulled her back into the castle as the sparkling transformation wave approached.

"You leave us alone!" Farmer shouted as she struggled to escape Stitcher's grasp to charge at the dragon.

"Farmer, get inside!" Gameknight shouted.

"Come on, Farmer, the transformation wave is coming," Stitcher said, pulling harder on the old woman.

Giving up her struggles, Farmer turned and headed back into the castle, her old legs moving slowly after the exertion.

"It's coming. Hurry!" the User-that-is-not-a-user shouted. "Get onto a block of obsidian!"

Gameknight looked through the iron bars and could see the transformation wave coming fast, the purple and yellow sparks lighting the ground with colorful, deadly embers. Water, grass, soil, trees . . . everything turned into the pale yellow cubes. He could almost feel the fabric of Minecraft cry out in despair as the landscape slowly died.

Stitcher first helped Farmer onto a dark obsidian cube, then turned and ran to her own, but Gameknight's heart sank when he saw the wave pass under the castle wall.

She's not going to make it, he realized.

Stitcher took two long strides and was about to jump to the dark stone when the sparkling wave touched her foot. She screamed as the transformation wave passed over her body. Gameknight watched as all the muscles in her body tensed as though she were overwhelmed with pain. Then she disappeared in a cloud of purple and insipid yellow particles as the wave moved over her body. When the particles finally disappeared, Gameknight could see his friend was gone. Standing in her place was an End Stone statue of Stitcher, her crimson curls now pale yellow.

"NOOOOO!" Gameknight screamed, but it was too late. She was gone.

"NOOOOO!" came a scream from the keep.

Gameknight could see Hunter peering out one of the windows.

As the wave passed through the castle's keep, the room instantly grew dark, Hunter's grief-stricken face disappearing in the gloom. The wave continued through the castle, flowing over the tall structure and turning the cobblestone walls and doors to End Stone, but leaving anything made of obsidian or on top of the dark blocks untouched. Gameknight did not watch the progress of the wave. He just stared at the statue of his friend, Stitcher.

When the wave had finally passed, the User-that-is-not-a-user stepped down and moved to Stitcher's frozen statue. Reaching up, he gently touched her stony curls, a look of terror frozen onto her young, petrified face.

Tears welled in his eyes, then streamed down his square cheeks. As if it were yesterday, Gameknight could remember that day in the Nether when he'd first met her after Malacoda had captured Hunter.

"You said, 'My name is Stitcher and I *will* be going with you. I dare you to try and stop me,'" Gameknight said to the statue. "I knew I could never stop you from doing anything that would help people. And now you've given your life to save someone you barely knew." He paused as tears streamed down his cheeks. "I wish it could have been me instead of you frozen here. I'm so sorry I failed you. . . . I'm so sorry."

Gameknight wanted to scream, wanted to just give up. But slowly the grief turned to rage as he thought about Herobrine out there, gloating over what he'd done.

He moved to the doors of the keep.

What am I going to find when I look inside? Gameknight thought. *What if it didn't work? What if my plan didn't protect everyone inside? Have I condemned all my friends to the same fate as Stitcher? Will this be my greatest failure?*

He pulled out his pickaxe and swung it into the End Stone door. It instantly shattered. He then hit the other door, smashing it into tiny yellow shards. The interior of the room was completely black, all the torches on the walls turned to stone, as well as the walls and glass windows.

Nervously, Gameknight leaned into the room, his eyes closed. He was afraid of what he was about to find, but knew he had to look. Slowly, he opened his eyes and found Hunter staring at him, her eyes filled with rage as tears ran down her cheeks.

"I couldn't stop her," Gameknight said. "I failed. . . . I killed Stitcher."

Hunter just stared at the frozen statue of her sister. She gritted her teeth, trying to stem the flow of tears, but the loss was too great. Finally, she broke down and sobbed, putting her arms around Gameknight's armored shoulders.

"Stitcher. . . . Stitcherrrrr!" she wailed as she was raked with emotion.

But then, a roar sounded from outside the walls of the castle. Both Gameknight and Hunter turned toward the sound, their tears replaced with fury.

"This isn't over yet," Gameknight growled.

"Not even close!" Hunter replied as she drew her bow and notched an arrow.

An army of angry villagers poured from the keep, Gameknight and Hunter in the lead, the dark obsidian floor having kept them all safe. They all glared at the statue of Stitcher, rage burning in their eyes. Knowing the plan, the NPCs spread out along the wall, hiding under the overhead walkway that ringed the castle wall.

Stepping up to the now End Stone doors, Gameknight reached into his inventory for his pickaxe, but Digger was already there, Crafter at his side. Swinging his tool, the big NPC smashed the brittle doors with a single hit, showering both of them with pale yellow shards. Crafter looked at his friend, then glanced at Stitcher. A tiny square tear trickled out of his bright blue eye as he looked up at Gameknight999. Gameknight placed a hand on his shoulder then shook his head.

"Save it for later my friend," Gameknight said.

Crafter nodded, then drew a dark chest from his inventory. Gameknight looked down at the item. It was dark purple, with streaks of green as well as the faintest presence of purple particles dancing about its surface.

"Are you sure about this?" Crafter asked, looking down at the chest.

"It's the only way," Gameknight replied. "It has to work, or Herobrine will win."

"OK," Crafter replied. "I'll be ready."

Gameknight nodded. Stepping through the doorway, Gameknight moved out in front of the castle, the other NPCs remaining hidden. The entire landscape had been changed into pale yellow End Stone: the trees, the flowing water . . . everything. Stepping out in the open, the User-that-is-not-a-user smiled when he saw a look of disbelief on Herobrine's dark face.

"You were careless when you were an NPC, Herobrine!" Gameknight yelled. "I see your arrogant carelessness has transferred to that pathetic dragon's body as well."

Drawing his two swords, Gameknight took a few more steps forward, then stopped and scratched a line in the ground.

"You have poisoned the land and hurt innocent people," the User-that-is-not-a-user yelled. "You're like a rabid animal that must be put down. You have brought The End to the Overworld, but in your foolish stupidity, you have actually brought your own end. You are nothing but a virus . . . and I am the cure."

Herobrine looked incredulous, his eyes wide with astonishment. Letting out an ear-splitting roar, he flapped his wings and leapt up into the air.

"Endermen, attack!" the dragon screamed, then swooped down toward Gameknight999.

With his two swords held firmly in his hands, Gameknight glanced over his shoulder at his friends within the castle, then gave the signal.

"FOR MINECRAFT!" the User-that-is-not-a user screamed, then turned and faced the dragon, who was diving straight toward him. "COME ON, HERO-BRINE. LET'S DANCE!"

CHAPTER 31

CAPTURING A DRAGON

Endermen disappeared in the distance and reappeared across from Gameknight999, but he was not concerned. Hundreds of NPCs poured from the castle gates. Each warrior stared at the frozen statue of Stitcher as they shot through the opening, a look of deadly determination on their square faces.

In the distance, Gameknight could see the three monster kings watching from their hilltops, apparently unwilling to join the fighting.

With yellow particles dancing around the endermen, the dark creatures attacked. They lunged at villagers, then disappeared, only to materialize behind them and attack their unprotected flank. But Gameknight had anticipated this and trained the NPCs how to fight back-to-back. The endermen were surprised to find blades on both sides of the villagers.

Shadowy monsters clashed with the NPCs, each scoring deadly hits on the other. Screeches of pain from the endermen pierced the air, but were accompanied by shouts of agony from the NPCs.

Gameknight had never seen such ferocious fighting before in Minecraft, but right now, endermen were not his concern. He had eyes for only the dragon diving toward him.

With pointed talons extended, the dragon reached out for Gameknight as he drew near. Rolling to his side, the User-that-is-not-a-user narrowly avoided being hit. As the dragon climbed into the sky, a flaming arrow shot up from the ground and hit the monster in the left wing.

"THAT WAS FOR STITCHER!" Hunter yelled.

A cheer erupted from the embattled NPCs.

The dragon roared, then flew across the landscape, looking for healing. Obsidian pillars had started to emerge up from the pale landscape, but they still needed to grow taller before any ender crystals would appear.

"Where you going, Herobrine?" Gameknight shouted. "ARE YOU AFRAID?"

The monster screamed its reptilian-like battle cry, then turned and dove for his enemy again. Running forward, Gameknight charged at the beast, both swords ready. When the monster drew near, it halted its dive. Turning, it swung its tail around, hoping to slam the pointed end into Gameknight999. But the User-that-is-not-a-user, having just fought a dragon when they'd saved Crafter, was ready.

He leapt high into the air as the tail passed underneath, the dark appendage smashing into NPCs and endermen. Landing on the ground, Gameknight sprinted toward the dragon, then jumped high into the air. Extending both his swords, he swung at the animal, grazing one of his legs and making him flash red.

Herobrine screamed, then beat his wings as he climbed into the sky. Facing downward, the monster spit his purple poison onto the ground again, trying to create another transformation wave that would convert the NPCs to stone.

But the splash of venom did nothing.

Gameknight laughed. "This is already part of The End," Gameknight shouted. "Your little trick won't work twice." He laughed at the dragon again. "Now, who is the fool?"

The dragon roared and dove toward Gameknight. Stepping backward, the User-that-is-not-a-user got ready to jump, but suddenly an enderman struck him in the side, knocking him down. Pain erupted through his body as the enderman moved closer.

"NO!" bellowed Herobrine. "HE IS MINE!"

The enderman bowed and turned to find another target.

The dragon charged forward as Gameknight was trying to stand, still dazed. More pain burst through his body as razor-sharp talons tore into his armor, the sharp points finding soft flesh. Before Gameknight could scream, Monkeypants charged at the dragon, his iron sword swinging down onto the dragon's shoulder. The monster roared in pain as the monkey's blade bit into his HP, making the beast flash red.

Flapping his mighty wings, the monster took to the air as Monkeypants helped his son to his feet. Looking up at Herobrine, Gameknight could see the monster's eyes blaze with anger and hatred, the creature overwhelmed with a desire to destroy his enemy.

"He's ready," Gameknight said to his father.

Looking back to the castle, Gameknight held up his swords and crossed them over his head. The signal brought another group of NPCs to the field of battle. But instead of bearing swords or bows, they held blocks of dirt and saplings. They ran out into the crazed battlefield, placing down blocks of dirt that extended out in front of the castle wall.

Knowing the plan, the warriors pushed the endermen away from the area so that the trap could be prepared. When their blocks had been placed and saplings planted, the NPCs drew their bows and focused their fire on the endermen, driving the dark creatures back from the area.

Moving to the center of the dirt, Gameknight put away his swords and stood with his arms outstretched. The warriors around him fought with crazed intensity, keeping the endermen far away. Glancing back at the castle entrance, he could see Treebrin and Grassbrin kneeling next to the dirt, ready.

"I'm tired of playing with you, Herobrine!" Gameknight shouted. "It's time we end this, face-to-face. That is . . . if you're not afraid of me."

The monster roared, then turned in a tight arc and headed for the ground. When he landed, he approached Gameknight999. As he neared, Gameknight moved backward. Reaching into his inventory, he pulled out an iron sword, but he fumbled with his grip on the hilt and it clattered to the pale yellow ground. Herobrine laughed as he glared at Gameknight, his eyes like intense lasers. Stepping backward, the User-that-is-not-a-user then stumbled and fell to the ground.

The dragon took advantage of the situation and moved forward with incredible speed . . . just as

Gameknight knew he would. Turning his head toward Grassbrin for just an instant, the User-that-is-not-a-user mouthed the word *Now*. Grassbrin instantly sent his crafting powers through the dirt, using every ounce of his strength and ability. Instantly, long blades of grass sprang up out of the ground, entangling the dragon's legs. As more grass wrapped around the monster, Treebrin plunged his hands into the ground, causing the saplings to burst out of the ground, forming a leafy canopy over the monster.

Herobrine's eyes flickered with doubt as he tried frantically to lift back off the ground, but it was too late.

Gameknight stood and ran for the trees. Jumping on top of the smaller ones, he sprinted to the top of the tallest oak, then turned and jumped on the dragon's back. At the same time, the NPCs dropped their swords and drew bows. Ignoring the endermen, they all fired on the dragon while Gameknight struck at the monster from above.

Hunter moved directly in front of the beast and stared into the monster's glowing eyes.

"THIS IS FOR STITCHER!" she shouted as she drew back a flaming arrow and fired, over and over again.

"AND FOR BUILDER . . ." another NPCs shouted.

"AND FOR WEAVER . . ."

"FOR CARVER . . ."

The litany of the dead flowed from the NPCs as those who had lost their lives were avenged.

The dragon roared in pain and surprise as its HP slowly ebbed away. The endermen attacked the NPCs, but by now they were too few. Some of the warriors turned and picked up their swords to engage the creatures, but Herobrine's fate was sealed. For a moment, Herobrine stopped his screams and concentrated intently, his body wrapped in a wreath of yellow particles, then his strength finally gave out.

"You may think you have defeated me, Gameknight999 . . . but I am not so easily deleted," Herobrine screamed with his final breaths.

The dragon then gave off one last great sorrowful wail as he started to glow bright from the inside. Shafts of light shot out from his scaly body as he glowed brighter and brighter. Gameknight, knowing what was about to happen, jumped off the monster's back and sprinted away. As he turned to face the monster, he saw Crafter run forward with a dark chest held before him, the lid thrown open.

Herobrine exploded in a blast of light and sound as his HP finally gave out, leaving behind a strange exit portal and balls of XP.

Instantly, the sparkling yellow particles that surrounded the endermen disappeared. The NPCs, following Gameknight's plan, stopped attacking the dark creatures and stepped back from them. Everyone looked away from the terrible monsters and moved clear of Herobrine's XP, which now littered the ground. Running forward, Crafter scooped up the glowing balls, using the dark chest to hold the poisonous spheres. In seconds, he had all the XP and closed the lid on the box.

Herobrine was gone.

CHAPTER 32

RETRANSFORMATION

Everyone cheered as the endermen teleported away. The shadowy creatures materialized back on the hill where the monster kings stood, disbelief on their hideous faces. NPCs ran to Gameknight, patting him on the back as they celebrated. But before Gameknight could say anything, he noticed a strange black mist start to emerge from the exit portal that stood where the Ender Dragon had perished. The curious fog moved slowly outward in all directions, a familiar sparkling look to it. Some of the NPCs saw it and moved away, but many either had their backs to the portal, or were in joyous celebration and didn't notice. Some of the villagers yelled to warn the others, but it was too late. The mist flowed past them harmlessly. Behind the mist, Gameknight could see the End Stone slowly dissolving, turning everything back to its original state, in this case flowing water.

As it approached, the User-that-is-not-a-user could see that the shimmering field was filled with stars, tiny white points of light that seemed to be cleansing the landscape.

"I know what that is," a voice said next to him.

Turning, Gameknight found his father standing at his side, his iron sword still in his hands.

"It's the portal," Monkeypants said as the wave passed under them. "You know, the field of stars that fills the exit portal. I remember it because I was staring into it right after Stitcher jumped in after defeating the dragon in The End."

"Stitcher!" Gameknight shouted, then turned and ran back into the castle. "Hunter, HUNTER!" Gameknight glanced about as he ran. When he located his friend, he yelled, "Come quick!"

She sprinted to his side as they ran past the moving dark fog. Shooting through the shattered gates, Gameknight ran to the End Stone statue of Stitcher and waited. Slowly, the retransformation wave moved under the castle wall and approached them. When the strange mist touched Stitcher's foot, a sparkling haze of stars enveloped her body. Ever so slowly, color began to flow back into the pallid statue, the pale yellow devoured by the shimmering field. Gameknight stared down at her as Stitcher's curls slowly blushed to a healthy red, and then the stars disappeared.

"Quick, get to the obsidian," Stitcher shouted. "The wave is coming!"

Gameknight smiled as he looked up at his friend.

"What are you two doing?" Stitcher exclaimed. "Quick, get on the blocks before the transformation wave—"

She stopped taking as she saw NPCs move into the village. They were all smiling as they looked at her, looks of joyous relief on their faces.

"What's happening?" the young girl asked.

"It's over," Hunter said. "Herobrine is gone, the war is over, and the land is changing back to the way it was again."

"What do you mean?" she asked.

"You were touched by Herobrine's wave and turned to End Stone," Gameknight explained. "But when we finally destroyed Herobrine, another wave came out of the exit portal and started changing everything back, including you. Likely all those NPCs in the other villages that were turned to stone will become alive again as well."

Hearing this, the villagers from other communities looked at each other, then ran for the crafting chamber and the minecart network that still ran throughout Minecraft, back toward the homes and the family members they thought they'd lost forever.

Crafter then pushed his way through the crowd, holding the dark chest carefully in his hands.

"So what is that chest?" Monkeypants asked.

"It's called an ender chest," Gameknight explained. "It's made from obsidian and an Eye of Ender. I figure that is the best way to hold Herobrine's evil XP until we can figure out a way to destroy it."

"So you mean . . . it's all over?" Stitcher said, still standing on the obsidian. "I missed the whole thing?"

"Don't worry," Gameknight replied as he reached out and helped her to the ground. "I'm sure there are a lot of people here who can tell you what happened."

"So what now?" Digger asked.

"First things first: let's get some doors back on the entrance," Gameknight commanded.

One of the NPCs pulled out a set of wooden doors and placed them in the obsidian wall. Satisfied they were safe for now, Gameknight sprinted to the top of the fortified wall. Across the battlefield, the retransformation wave was moving outward, leaving healthy grassy blocks in its wake.

The endermen, seeing the wave approach, all teleported away, leaving the monster kings alone on the End Stone hill. Not waiting to see what happened when the wave reached them, Xa-Tul and Reaper turned their monstrous horses and sprinted into the night, leaving Feyd to stand there glaring back at them.

"Your Maker's time is over," Gameknight yelled. "And your time is over, as well. When we find you again, you will receive the same fate as Herobrine so that Minecraft can finally be at peace."

The king of the endermen growled as he glared at his enemy.

Just then, Digger moved next to the User-that-is-not-a-user, a curious look on his face.

"Digger, what is it?" Gameknight asked.

"Something has changed," the big NPC said.

Reaching into his inventory, he pulled out a second pickaxe and held them both over his head. More NPCs came up onto the fortified walls and stood at their side. They, too, reached into their inventory and each pulled out a second weapon. Gameknight looked at his comrades and smiled.

"Looks like we have a few more surprises for you, Feyd," the User-that-is-not-a-user yelled. "Why don't you come on down here and face justice?"

"You don't frighten me, *Gameknight999*," Feyd said with a sneer. "I shall be looking forward to that meeting. If you think you have seen the last of my endermen, or me, then you are truly the Fool. For now, it is farewell, but rest assured, we will be locked in battle soon. You can count on that."

Just before the retransformation wave reached him, the shadowy creature disappeared, then materialized on the exit portal just outside the castle. Reaching up, the king of the endermen grabbed the dragon's egg that sat atop the bedrock portal, then disappeared in a cloud of purple particles.

"At least he's gone," Digger said at Gameknight's side.

"Yeah, for now," Hunter added from the other side. "But I have the feeling he'll be back."

Gameknight glanced at Digger, then looked at the other NPCs on the wall, all of them holding two weapons.

"What happened with the weapons?" he asked.

"I don't know," Digger replied. "I could just feel that something changed. Maybe it was a software update, or maybe it was the retransformation wave. Who knows?"

"You're upset about it?" Hunter said.

"The last thing we need is another surprise," Gameknight replied. He put away his weapons, then looked around at the village and landscape. "Herobrine did some significant damage to the village wall," Gameknight said. "We have a lot of work to do to make the village safe again."

He slid down a ladder to the ground, then moved toward Crafter.

"I think we should put the ender chest in the top floor of my castle," Gameknight explained. "We'll wall it in with more obsidian and hope that keeps him contained . . . for now."

"I'll help, I'll help," Herder said.

Crafter nodded, then took off with the dark chest, Herder running close behind. Gameknight and Monkeypants followed as the villagers started the long task of repairing the landscape and village with Digger directing their labors.

Running into the keep, they crossed the obsidian floor and took the stairway that led upward into the tower. With each floor, the tower became narrower and narrower. At its base, the tower was maybe twenty blocks across, but at its peak was only six blocks wide. This would be the resting place of the ender chest.

Crafter carefully placed the chest in the center of the room, then backed away cautiously. For some reason, Herder moved close to the box and leaned down, pressing his ear to the chest.

"I can almost hear him in there," the lanky NPC said. "He's scared. I can feel it."

"What do you mean you can feel it?" Gameknight asked.

"I could feel him when he was a dragon, and I can still sense him, somehow, in my mind," Herder replied. "He's confused and scared and doesn't know what's going to happen to him."

"I don't care what he feels," Gameknight snapped. "Don't be tricked into giving him any sympathy. That monster would have destroyed us all if given the chance. You stay away from this chest."

Herder nodded his head, his long black hair draped over his face, but he did not look at Gameknight; his eyes were still fixed on the chest.

"Herder, did you hear me?" Gameknight said.

He reached out and turned the boy away from the ender chest so that he could face him. Looking deep into his eyes, Gameknight though he saw a dreamy, confused look on Herder's face. But as he pulled him farther away from the chest, the lanky NPC seemed to look normal again.

Herder can be so strange sometimes, Gameknight thought but still wondered about that look in his eyes. It wasn't right.

"We'll post guards at the doors and make sure the ender chest is kept safe," Crafter said. "No one will be able to get in or out without us knowing about it."

"I'll put some of my wolves on guard as well," Herder said.

"That sounds good," the User-that-is-not-a-user said. "But for now, let's get out of here. Being close to that monster gives me the creeps."

Moving to the door, the trio left the ender chest in the dark room and went back to the court-yard of the castle. When they reached the ground floor, Gameknight found his father waiting at the entrance to the keep, Hunter and Stitcher at his side.

"Well?" Hunter asked.

"He's safely tucked away up there," Crafter said. "We'll need some guards to keep him safe."

"And my wolves," Herder added.

"Yes, and your wolves," Crafter affirmed, giving the boy a smile.

"I'll go find some," Herder said as he pulled out a bone and ran to the castle gates.

"That boy is certainly motivated," Monkeypants said.

"That's for sure," Gameknight agreed.

"So what about you two?" Stitcher asked.

The User-that-is-not-a-user looked down at her and smiled, then turned and faced his father.

"I guess we should be . . ." Gameknight said but stopped when his father raised a hand to stop his son.

Monkeypants looked at Gameknight and then looked at the NPCs, his son's best friends. He then looked around at the solid castle wall, then glanced over at the half-destroyed village wall next to it.

"You may be stubborn about refusing to give up, but I'm obsessed with seeing things completed," Monkeypants said. "That's how I get my inventions done so quickly. I can't stop until they are complete. Look around you."

Gameknight scanned the castle grounds. It had fared well through the battle, but the village was in a shambles. Half-destroyed archer towers loomed over the shattered battlements, evidence of Herobrine's violence; scars that needed mending.

"We can't just leave with all this damage," Monkeypants said. "Never leave a job half-complete. That's my motto."

Stitcher smiled, then moved to the monkey and gave him a big hug. Hunter, too, looked at Gameknight's father and grinned, then gave the User-that-is-not-a-user a smile.

"We could use the help," Hunter said. "There is certainly a lot to do."

"Then let's get to it," Monkeypants said. "I have some ideas for a few inventions that might make things a bit easier . . . maybe some automated farming to start with."

"That sounds extremely interesting," Crafter said. "We should discuss this."

"Well, here's what I'm thinking . . ." Monkeypants said as he walked off with Crafter listening intently.

In the distance, Gameknight could hear the howls of wolves and smiled, knowing Herder had found some more "friends."

"Come on, let's get the village wall repaired," Stitcher said. "Then maybe we can finish our archery match . . . even though you were losing."

"I was just getting warmed up," Gameknight complained.

"Yeah, right," Hunter said. "I've seen you shoot, and you don't stand a chance against my little sister."

"We'll see," Gameknight replied as the trio headed off for the village.

Behind them, the terrible XP infected with Herobrine's AI virus sat in the ender chest . . . waiting.

MINECRAFT SEEDS

A book warp room has been added to the Gameknight999 Minecraft server for each book I've written. In this room, you'll find a hologram floating above the wall for each Gameknight999 book, with signs showing the chapter and which biome it will send you to. Just step up and click the button, and you can see the biome that I was looking at when I wrote the book. Many people have enjoyed going to the ocean monument to face the Elder Guardian or have voyaged through Malacoda's fortress in the Nether.

If you can't get onto the server, I've also provided seed values and coordinates for you to use in Minecraft so that you can see these areas in your own single-player world.

I hope you enjoy these warps. Readers from many countries have tried them out and seem to like exploring them.

Book Warp room on
Gameknight999's server
Server IP: Go to www.markcheverton.com and
click on the Minecraft Servers tab

Chapter 1:	Sunflower biome	-252953672 x: -342, z: 358
Chapter 2:	Oak forest	-2085488970
Chapter 3:	Savannah village	-74179593399 4633340 x: 261, z: 113
Chapter 4:	Crafter's village	see Game-knight999's server
	Crafting chamber	see Game-knight999's server
Chapter 7:	Desert village	-22255155669 1018 x: -215, z: -857
Chapter 10:	Frozen river biome	6992
Chapter 11:	Grassland village	-22255155669 1018

NOTE FROM THE AUTHOR

I've come to appreciate the incredible creativity of the many readers who have submitted images and stories to my website, www.markcheverton. com. A relatively new feature is the creation and public access to Gameknight999's Minecraft server; you can find the IP address on my website easily. If you can't find it, please send me an email. On his server, I've been able to watch the creativity in real time and have been amazed at what I've seen. A village sprouted up out of nowhere, with incredible houses and shops created from people's imaginations. I really like the pet shops and the floating bases with their trading centers, crops, and monster grinders. In the creative world, the pixel art and architecture slowly emerging from the plots is a testament to the creativity and incredible imaginations of kids from across the world. If you check the warp room, you'll find a portal to Crafter's village. Of course, beneath the tall watchtower, you'll find a passage to the crafting chamber. Next to the village is Gameknight's castle, complete with the obsidian wall. Be careful if you go to the top room of the keep; you may find a dangerous chest there. In addition, you can find Malacoda's fortress in the

Nether as well as many other incredible creations.

All the additions to the server have been a wonderful process to watch, and a special thank-you goes out to quadbamber and LBEGaming on YouTube for their help setting all this up. Their video tutorials on server plug-ins and mods have been incredibly helpful, so check them out if you need help. Look for Gameknight999 and me, Monkeypants271, out there on our server. If you're brave enough, maybe you can challenge us to a game of spleef or paintball—but only if you dare!

Everyone: keep reading, keep writing, keep creating, and, of course, watch out for creepers.

Mark

DO YOU LIKE FICTION FOR MINECRAFTERS?

Check out these unofficial Minecrafter adventures from Sky Pony Press!

Invasion of the Overworld
MARK CHEVERTON

Battle for the Nether
MARK CHEVERTON

Confronting the Dragon
MARK CHEVERTON

Trouble in Zombie-town
MARK CHEVERTON

The Quest for the Diamond Sword
WINTER MORGAN

The Mystery of the Griefer's Mark
WINTER MORGAN

The Endermen Invasion
WINTER MORGAN

Treasure Hunters in Trouble
WINTER MORGAN

Available wherever books are sold!

EXCERPT FROM GAMEKNIGHT999 VS. HEROBRINE

As they entered the pass, Gameknight999 felt a strange unease spread through his body. This would be a great place for an ambush, and even though Crafter said Two-Sword Pass was a secret only known to the NPCs, he'd learned not to underestimate Herobrine or his monster kings. Stopping for a moment, he glanced nervously over his shoulder, then peered up along the sheer stone walls that hugged the narrow corridor. Straining all of his senses, he scanned every aspect of their surroundings, looking for the angry red eyes of spiders, and listening for the sorrowful moans of zombies or the clattering of skeleton bones. He sensed nothing but a gentle wind that caressed his square cheeks.

"Are you coming, or are you planning on staying for some kind of extended vacation?" Hunter asked sarcastically.

"Hunter!" Stitcher snapped. "Why do you always have to be . . ."

"You're always lecturing me," the older sister interrupted. "Have you ever noticed that? I'm tired of . . ."

"Stop arguing!" shouted Digger, his voice echoing off the stone walls of the pass.

This silenced the two girls, but they still glared at each other. Crafter walked forward and placed a hand on each, calming the sisters.

"We are getting close to our goal and will soon be rid of our evil cargo," Crafter said calmly. "I'm sure Herobrine senses this somehow and is working hard to divide us. He would love nothing more than to have us all turn on each other. You must remember that we are a family and everyone here would do anything to help another. Our bonds are forged from trust and our willingness to always be there to help." The young NPC's voice rose in volume as he stood a bit taller. "We are stronger than Herobrine's irritating whine will ever be, and nothing will stop us from dropping that ender chest into The Abyss." He cast his bright blue eyes to Herder and glared at the dark box under his arm, then glanced at his other companions. "We must stick together and keep trying to work together. Remember, each of us are relying on the other and no one is alone."

The sisters nodded to Crafter and looked apologetically at each other, then smiled.

"Let's get this done," Digger boomed as he pulled out his pair of iron pickaxes and started forward, the rest of the party following close behind.

The pass was maybe six blocks wide, at some places wider, at others narrower. Sheer stone walls stretched up from the ground, making Gameknight feel as if he were in a curvy tunnel whose ceiling was out of sight. The light grew dim as the hills blocked if there were a hundred people in their party . . . Gameknight wished that were the case.

Suddenly, the piercing whine from the ender chest increased in volume tenfold. Stitcher yelled out in pain as she tried to cover her ears with her hands, but it did no good.

"Monsters must be coming," Crafter shouted. "Run!"

The party sprinted forward, following the winding pathway. Ahead was a sharp bend in the pass, but when they bolted around the corner, everyone skidded to a stop. Ahead of them were half a dozen spiders blocking the pass, with another six climbing down the walls.

Before anyone could think, Gameknight charged forward, his diamond sword in his right hand, his iron sword in his left. Purple waves of enchanted light painted the walls of the pass as he crashed into the monsters.

"FOR MINECRAFT!" the User-that-is-not-a-user yelled, his swords slashing at the dark fuzzy creatures.

out the rays of the sun, putting the party in complete shadow. The only time the pass saw sunlight was at high noon, when the sun was directly overhead. But with the sun still far from the horizon, they would likely be through the pass before dusk.

Ahead, Two-Sword Pass turned to the left, then zigzagged around large piles of sand, finally curving to the right. Glancing over his shoulder, Gameknight found the entrance was now completely hidden, the exit still concealed from view. The curving path made it difficult to see very far ahead or behind the party, and it made the User-that-is-not-a-user feel uneasy.

"I don't like this," Gameknight said as he drew his enchanted diamond sword from his inventory. "We can't see anything."

Hunter nodded and pulled out her bow, but then put it away; the curving pathway made the weapon relatively ineffective. If they had to battle any monsters, it would be up close and personal, and that was sword work.

"Everyone get ready," the User-that-is-not-a-user said. "I have a bad feeling about this."

Just then, a clicking sound echoed off the steep rocky walls. Gameknight wasn't sure if it had been his imagination or just a trick of the wind.

"What was that?" he asked.

His voice echoed off the stone walls and reflected back to him. On its return, his voice sounded thin and scared.

Everyone stopped and stood motionless . . . listening. As they stood there, Gameknight scanned the sheer walls that boxed them in, but there was nothing . . . just stone.

They continued to move forward. Every step echoed off the curving walls, making it sound as